ALSO BY LAURA DALEO

Immortal Kiss

The Vow

The Vampire Within

The Soul Collector

The Doll

Once We Were Witches

Bound by Blood

By

Laura Daleo

AUTHOR LAURA DALEO

Published in the United States by Author Laura Daleo, San Diego, California

Print ISBN: 9780997846140

ebook ISBN: 9780997846157

To Claudette and David,

many thanks for making my vision come alive

CHAPTER 1

The wind howled into the dark night, chilling my freshly warmed skin. As I stood at the rim of the ocean's cliffs, listening to the whispering waves, I focused on my victim's vacant stare and wiped his blood from my lips. A single drop tarnished his forehead, and I snatched it up with my tongue. Lowering my head, I whispered, "Forgive me, dear mortal, for though I share your love of life, I must rob you of yours so that I may survive." Hugging his cold torso against my chest, I kissed his cheek and then tossed him over the cliffs into the pounding surf.

The platinum moonlight shimmered across the restless water and bounced off of his body. The waves swelled, swallowing him whole and erasing him from the mortal world, but I couldn't walk away. I owed the mortal a glimmer of respect; after all, he'd sacrificed his precious blood to feed me. Like a mourner at his grave, I clasped my hands in front of me and stared ahead in silence. I lingered for only a moment longer as a personal task; in truth, it was more of an important ritual, one of self-pity, drunkenness, and shame which required my devotion. This very night marked the fifth anniversary of the spell cast upon Amon, forcing him to bid me farewell. Faithfully, I waited for his return, and with each passing year the hole in my heart grew wider, leaving my immortal soul a bit emptier, and the wedge between Philippe and I a bit deeper.

Turning my back on the sea, I drifted along the cliff's path, crossed the deserted street, and headed for home. As I entered the front door, I cocked my head and listened with my vampire ears. My ritual was private and for me alone. No interruptions. No distractions. No nothing, and especially not Philippe. Again I took notice of the house. Not a single sound made its way into my ears. Not trusting in them solely, I closed my eyes, lifted my arms, and spread my fingers. No spike in my pulse. No surge in my veins. Philippe's blood didn't stir; but then, could his presence be masked?

I opened my eyes, slipped off my shoes, and tiptoed across the foyer toward the wine cellar door hidden beneath the staircase. As I descended the steps, I welcomed the cold of the floor against my bare feet. After all, mine wasn't a body composed of warmth. Beneath my flesh rushed an icy scarlet river, which required human blood to generate any heat.

As I wandered along the cellar rows, I caressed the black and gold bottle necks, searching for Amon's favorite vintage. Several steps ahead, it lay before my gaze. I slowed, but my breath quickened. I removed it from its slot, pressing it to my lips. Amon's emerald-green eyes, jet-black hair, and handsome face flashed before my eyes. Memories of the dreadful night we said goodbye flooded my mind. Goosebumps pinched at my flesh. I reached out, grasping empty air. His reflection shattered, leaving me alone all over again. A spark of madness singed my brain, and I slumped against the cellar wall, gripping the bottle, whimpering. The walls seemed to close in on me. I needed air.

Leaping to my feet, I rushed from the room. I didn't stop running until the beach's soft blanket of silver sand tickled my toes. My knees buckled and I sank, sitting inches from the waves. I popped the cork and filled my mouth with wine. I quickly drained the bottle, anesthetizing my pain. I fell backward, spreading my legs and arms across the sand, staring into the night sky. Amon's image floated above, torturing me. I brushed my fingers over my heart before they fell away and into the sand. "I failed you," I murmured, gripping a shifting handful of sand. I sat up, flinging it with force and shouting, "I failed you." Tears stung behind my eyelids, and I hung my head so they could fall. For hours, it seemed, I cried...then slowly, very slowly, the wine took hold. I lay blissfully drunk, the empty bottle by my side and my ritual performed.

Footsteps approached, a shadow creeping over me and blocking out the moon. My pulse thumped under my skin. I knew who it was. He always found me, but I didn't acknowledge him. I kept my gaze focused on the stars.

"Drunk again, Beth," Philippe said rather than asked, blowing out a groan.

Only then did I meet his gray-blue eyes. He stood over me with his hands on his hips. This was my way every year. Why did he continue to judge me? He had no right, the Amon imposter. If I chose to drown my pain in wine, then so be it. I didn't need his permission. Deliberately, I giggled and said, "Very drunk."

He glanced over his shoulder and then back at me. "It's close to sunrise. Come home."

I waved him off. "To hell with the sun. Go home if you want. I'm fine right here."

He looked away from me, pursing his lips and shaking his head. "You know, this woe-is-me attitude of yours is getting pretty old." He slowly turned his head toward me, a stone-cold expression plastered on his face. "In fact, I'm quite sick of it."

I sat up and scowled at him. "Don't mock my pain. Let me feel wretched and miserable on this night."

He narrowed his eyes and arched his brow. "The promise no longer threatens us. We have everything we ever wanted. We should be having the time of our lives, but it isn't just the one night. You live in a constant state of drunkenness and depression. Amon isn't coming back. Get over it."

"How can you? Of all things…" I stammered and then collected myself. "I'm not going to dignify that with a response."

He knelt beside me, brushing sand from my forehead. "Did you ever think the spell lifted? That he made another choice?" He leaned in closer and whispered into my ear, "Perhaps he chose Hathor."

As he spoke, his words seared through my chest, leaving a deep, agonizing wound in my heart. I shoved him away. "When did you become so cruel?

He swept an arm through the air in exasperation. "About the same time you chose Amon over me."

I ground my teeth together yet kept my tone calm. "I never chose Amon over you. I chose you because I thought you *were* Amon."

His stony expression twisted into a painful grimace. "Now who's being cruel?"

I slumped forward, shaking my head. "I don't want to fight anymore."

He joined our hands and softly said, "I don't either."

I met his eyes. "Then accept me, the vampire I am today, binding ritual and all."

His posture stiffened, and he released my hands. "I can't do that." His glare was harsh. "I'm your husband. I'm here. I've picked up the pieces for the last five years." He held up his palms. "Where has Amon been? With Hathor. You need to accept that."

Words rushed out of my mouth like air escaping from a balloon. "What I accept, what I know, is that Amon's blood rushes through my veins, binding us as one. His heartbeat is my heartbeat, his breath is my breath, and his soul is my soul. I can't change that. It can't be undone. It's who I am now. Maybe you need to accept that."

His eyes dulled, and his tone fell flat. "Maybe, but you love him. That's a harder pill to swallow."

My breath hitched, and tears moistened my eyes. "But I love you too. I never stopped."

He ran his hands over his face and then through his hair. "This is all wrong, and there's nothing I can do."

"I'm sorry," I whispered.

His whole body trembled, and then he reached for my hand again. "I *can* make you happy again. Let me in. Let me show you."

Pulling away, I lowered my eyes. "I...I don't trust you."

His shoulders caved, and he looked down at his feet.

Subtle warmth crept up behind me, and I turned to find its source. Tiny pinpricks of heat darted across my skin. "The sun!"

Philippe's head jerked up. "No," he uttered, and with vampire swiftness leapt to his feet.

I stood, swayed, and then fell backward.

His eyes bulged, and he yanked me to my feet. "Damn it, Beth, run!"

I glanced over my shoulder. The orange ball of flames inched over the sea's edge, taking possession of the sapphire-blue sky. Within seconds, daggers of light pierced my eyes. I threw up my hand, shielding my face. It went up in flames. Sizzling heat torched my fingers. The stench of burnt flesh stung my nostrils—*my* burnt flesh. I doubled over, screaming in pain. Philippe flung his jacket over me, swept me up in his arms, and bolted for the house with preternatural speed. He nearly ripped the door from its hinges as he thrust it open, carrying us inside. He rushed me up the stairs and into our bedroom, and from there pushed me inside the bathroom. He shoved me under the shower, jumping in after me. Frantically he cranked the faucet, dousing our dangerously feverish bodies with cold water, lessening the stinging in my skin. I sagged against him, releasing a pent-up breath.

"We were lucky," he said, shutting off the water.

I brushed tears off my face. "We were careless."

He took a step back, shaking water from his hair. "We? You were the one who lost track of time because of your ritual, not to mention being completely hammered. Once again, I had to come find you. What if I hadn't? What then, Beth?"

I bit the inside of my cheek and glared at him but didn't say a word.

He glared back.

Complete silence filled the room.

After a minute or two he let out a groan of frustration and shed his wet clothes, tossing them carelessly onto the chair. As he pulled on a pair of pajama bottoms, he switched off the light as if I weren't even there.

My muscles clenched, and nasty words raced up my throat. It took all my will to swallow them whole. Instead of ranting, I turned my back on him and left the room. In the hallway I balled my hands into fists, my fingernails biting into my palms. How dare he speak to me like that and then just ignore me? My rapid strides down the corridor expanded the distance between us. I came to a dead stop in front of the room I'd stayed in on my first night in this house. I pushed open the door and stepped inside. My mind raced backward, conjuring up memories. I'd found Philippe's bedroom that next morning, been brave enough to kiss him as he'd slept, and then fled back into this very room to lie breathless across the bed. So much had changed since that long-ago night.

What had happened to that lovesick girl? She'd been used, lied to, and betrayed, that's what. We were fools trying to hang onto a love based on deception.

Shaking off the past, I gripped the doorknob and let the door slam shut. I moped my way into the bathroom to strip off my wet clothes, draping them carefully over the tub while purposely avoiding my reflection in the mirror. I climbed naked into the bed, cuddling up to a pillow, and whispered, "Amon, come back to me."

I awoke feeling somewhat rested, with the crushing weight of the dreadful anniversary gone. Yet my loneliness lingered, tormenting my immortal heart. I tumbled out of bed, pulled on my damp clothes, and snuck down the hallway to our bedroom. Placing my ear against the door, I listened. Not a sound came from within the room. When I turned the knob it creaked, and I cringed. I peered into the room as I pushed the door all the way open. Philippe was gone, and I released a breath of relief. I hurried inside and into the closet, ripping clothes off hangers and snagging a pair of boots from the shelf. I dressed hastily and then fled the room.

Near the bottom of the stairs I ran into Betty. Her motherly expression stopped me at the last step. "Come here, Beth."

There was no way of getting around her. Like a scolded child, I crept into her line of sight.

She cupped my cheeks, searching my eyes. "I know this is probably none of my business, but I think of you as a daughter, and it kills me to see you suffering. Talk to me."

I stared into her kind eyes and softly said, "I can't."

She dropped her hands and took a step back, eyeing me shrewdly. "You can, child. Yes, I'm loyal to Philippe, but that doesn't mean you can't confide in me."

I wanted to tell her. I wanted to blurt it all out. I really did. *The binding ritual changed everything. I'm different now. Philippe's different now. Our love is different now, and Amon stands between us.* But the words never escaped my mouth. I pushed her aside gently and said again, "I can't. I'm sorry."

I ran out of the house and into the street. As our home vanished from my sight, my pace slowed and I strolled along the sidewalk, actually humming.

"Excuse me, can you help me?" The male voice came out of nowhere. "I'm looking for Ocean Boulevard."

My vision sharpened, searching the street. A sandy-haired man sitting in a parked car fell into my sight. I eyed his mouthwatering, pulsating jugular and licked my lips.

He jumped out of his car and stepped onto the curb. "Can you help me?" he asked, holding up a map.

Tremendous blood hunger rumbled through my veins, weakening my fading human loyalties. Arching a brow, I said in a silken voice, "Come closer. Let me see the map."

"Oh, sure," he said, jogging over to me and handing it over.

His scent rushed up my nostrils, tickling my brain and sending my heartbeat raging. Saliva flooded my mouth, and I tingled all over. Gracefully I took the map, spreading my most inviting smile over my lips—and knowing full well where Ocean Boulevard was. For the moment I simply wanted to stand close to him, to get a good whiff and let it send ripples of pleasure through me. The pleasure of the undead—the pleasure formed from blood.

"Do you know it?" he asked, looking at me with raised brows. "Stupid GPS has me driving in circles."

I could have lied, said I hadn't a clue and lingered next to him, drowning in his intoxicating fragrance, but he wasn't a pet I could toy with. He was a human being, something I'd once been. Gazing at him, it suddenly occurred to me I didn't have to steal his life when scores of humans lined the walls of Bloodthirst eager to be tasted. Like a bee collecting pollen, I could float from human to human extracting blood. It was a brilliant plan; but it was a social establishment with riotous behavior I'd once sworn I would never take part in. But that had been then, and this was now.

Pointing up the street while handing the map back, I rattled off, "Make your first left on Cove Court, a right on Reef, and then Ocean Boulevard is a few blocks down."

Smashing the map between his hands, he responded, "Thank you," and then turned to run back to his car.

I stood still, waiting for him to leave. As he pulled away from the curb, I blasted off the ground, propelling upward and whizzing through the night sky. Cool air whipped through my hair and nipped at my cheeks. I laughed out loud and spread my arms wide. Why Philippe chose not to fly was beyond me. It came so naturally, as if I'd been born a bird. I would never give it up, never.

Bloodthirst's floating red neon letters flickered in the darkness below me. I slowed my descent as I approached the ground. Seconds before the golden door was locked, I slipped inside. The familiar gust of freezing air caressed my skin as I roamed past the dark red walls toward the circular black-velvet booths and all the warm bodies full of blood. Their delightful coppery scent made my head spin. I swayed and shuddered, longing for a taste. The routine opening speech rumbled through my ears.

"Welcome," the MC began in his hypnotizing voice. "The doors to Bloodthirst are locked. The club has a few simple rules. Vampires are free to come and go as they please. Humans may exit Bloodthirst at any time; however, once you vacate the premises, you will not be allowed to reenter. If a vampire approaches you, you may choose to accept or refuse their kiss. If you refuse, the vampire must respect your wishes and walk away. We will guarantee your safety." His ruby lips spread into a clichéd devilish grin. "On the other hand, if you accept, you do so at your own risk, so choose wisely." He waved his hand in the air. "Let the events begin."

The crowd scattered but I stood still, fidgeting with the zipper on my jacket. How did I ask for a kiss? Should I be straightforward or subtle? Skimming over the herd of immortals and mortals, I cocked my head, eavesdropping on their conversations. Numerous excited voices throbbed inside my ears: *"I want you," "Take me," "May I drink?" "Yes,"*

"Will you accept my kiss?" *"Absolutely."* Didn't seem so hard. I took a step forward.

"Silly Beth," Margarete said, appearing out of nowhere. Brushing her long raven-colored hair over her shoulders, she snickered, and then the grin disappeared from her cherry-red lips. "You need not lift a finger. Humans will fall all over one another to have your fangs in their throats. None will be able to resist your beauty." She glanced over her shoulder. "See, here comes a fool now," she whispered, vanishing and leaving me alone.

A young man with chocolate-brown skin, long dreadlocks, and crystal-clear hazel eyes rushed up in front of me. "Will you kiss me?" he blurted out.

Margarete was right. Smiling in satisfaction, I stared at him only a moment before answering. "Yes, I will."

A ruddy blush spread over his face. "Cool," he said, narrowing the gap between us.

He closed the distance between us, and his soft, supple lips were pressing against mine. The jarring beat of his heart pumping blood through his veins set me afire. Sweat coated my palms, and my fangs tingled with delight. Inching my mouth down his neck, I stopped at the base of his throat. Saliva flooded my mouth right before I stabbed his throbbing jugular. Hot, salty blood squirted over my tongue. I swallowed, shuddered, and swallowed again, slower this time. The metallic sweetness of his blood was a delight to taste.

He cried out and pressed up against me. His arms wrapped around my waist, and he moaned in my ear. A low growl, as from a panther cornering its prey, rose from the pit of my abdomen. The power of the bloodlust tempted me, but I hadn't come to kill. Inside my head I set a timer, allowing myself one minute of bliss, and then I'd let him go. Twenty seconds sailed by as I clung to him, draining away. Forty seconds later, my eyelashes fluttered in ecstasy, and I swayed in his arms. Floating along on the thrill of his blood, I dug my fangs in deeper, just as the one-minute alarm bell rang inside my brain. Refusing to comply with my own rule, I clung to him tightly, trembling all over. Sixty-five seconds passed. *Release him.* I tried to pull my head back, but my shoulders bent forward, attaching to him like a magnet to metal. The seventy seconds mark hit. *Stop now!* Grumbling out a frustrated breath, I shoved him backward, shattering the spell of his blood.

In a high, breathless voice, he managed, "That was friggin' awesome. I want to do it again."

I dug my fingers into his arm, pulling him close. "Vampires here will not be so generous with your life and let you live as I have. Leave now. You've had your fun."

Balling his hands into fists, he thrust them into the air. "No way!" He turned and dashed off into the crowd.

I waved him off. "Idiot." Hunger still twisted my gut, demanding my attention. Weaving between the humans, I homed in on eager heartbeats, searching for my next meal.

Adhering to my sixty-second rule, it took eight bodies to satisfy my appetite. My body ached as blood coursing through my veins burned with a thirst for alcohol. Pursuing the therapy of wine, I headed to the bar. I leaned forward, resting my elbows on the counter and eyeballing the collection of bottles stacked on the shelf.

A bartender with a gleaming, shaved head approached me. Spreading his ruby-red lips into a charming smile while flashing his fangs, he asked, "What can I get for you, beautiful?"

I gave a nod toward a particular bottle. "Pinot Grigio, please."

He winked at me. "One glass coming right up."

I shook my head and raised my hand. "No, no, no. I want the bottle."

He stared for a moment before bobbing his head. "Will do." He snatched the clear glass bottle filled with light gold liquid off the shelf, set it on the bar, and popped the cork. Handing me the bottle and a glass, he said, "On the house."

It was my turn to stare.

He looked me up and down before giving me a heartfelt look. "Pretty vamp like you shouldn't have to drown her sorrows in wine."

My shoulders slumped, and I blew out a sigh. Giving him a half smile, I replied, "Thank you. I appreciate your kindness." Without hesitation, I scooped up the bottle and glass.

"Anytime."

I wandered until I could claim an empty booth tucked away in the far corner of the club. After filling my glass to the rim, I raised it to my lips and took a generous swallow. While the delicate flavors of citrus rolled down my throat, I shuddered with delight. Closing my eyes, I rested my head against the back of the booth, allowing the alcohol to take hold. I took another swig, then another, before finally knocking back what remained. I latched onto the bottle, spilling wine on the table as I refilled the glass. Laughing, I shrugged my shoulders, then drank. Sinking into the booth with the bottle now glued to my lips, I gorged on wine. Numbing pleasure crept over me. A slackened smile spread across my lips. Pushing the empty bottle away, I went limp, my arms dangling at my sides.

"What a drunken sight you are, Beth," Margarete said, rolling her eyes at me. Turning my head in her direction, I squinted, forcing my eyes to focus.

Her violet eyes hardened with disapproval. "Shall I summon Philippe to come and collect you?"

I lunged out and grabbed her arm. "No. Don't." I released her and, holding my head high, pushed myself upright. "I can take care of myself."

She crossed her arms over her chest and huffed. "Right now you couldn't even find your way out of that booth."

"I most certainly can," I assured her in my most confident tone. Scooting along the seat, I swayed and sat still.

A burst of laughter flew out of her mouth. "See. You're smashed. If you don't want me to call Philippe, then let me summon Caleb. Someone has to help you."

"I'll see that she gets home safely," Ptah offered, coming up behind Margarete.

His voice raised my spirits, and I clasped my hands to my chest, praying he had news of Amon.

Margarete quickly lowered her head and stepped out of his way. "As you wish, Supreme Ruler."

He lifted her chin and smiled at her, his almond-colored eyes glinting under the club lights. "Dear child, I am no ruler." He let out a laugh and placed his hands upon his chest. "Though I'll admit, I am flattered you see me as such."

Margarete flashed him a jittery smile, gave me a fleeting nod, and then scurried away.

His gaze lingered, following her retreat; then he shrugged his shoulders and turned back to me. Before sliding into the booth, he gave me a thorough once-over. "She's right. You're in no shape to see yourself home."

I ignored his concern, obsessed with the words that rushed out of my mouth. "Any news of Amon?"

He pressed his lips together in a hard line and swept a hand across his neatly trimmed beard. "My trip to The Council's haven was futile. Kohath watches their blood vials day and night; yet, they remain dark, not even the slightest flicker. It appears Isis's magic has camouflaged them."

I dug my palms into my temples, sighing heavily. "Will this never end? Philippe and I are at each other's throats. Must I continue on like this year after year?"

He rested his hand on my shoulder. "Amon will return to you. You must hold on to your faith."

I drew in my brows and tightened my jaw. "I'm not so sure anymore. I mean, it's been five years. Can a spell last so long?"

"What is it, Beth? What happened to sway your resolve?"

I glanced at the empty wine bottle, wishing for just a drop more. Facing Ptah, I twisted my hands together in my lap as I spoke. "Philippe believes the spell ended and that Amon chose Hathor."

A deep crease cut through his forehead. "Nonsense. Philippe speaks from a jealous heart." He leaned across the table to give my hand a squeeze. "Amon loves you more than life's blood." His face softened. "These years without Amon have been disheartening and have taken their toll on everyone, me as well. I have searched the world...literally. While it seems as though Isis's magic has erased all evidence of her, Osiris, Hathor, and Amon, the battle is far from over and we cannot surrender. We must be strong. Believe, Beth. Faith is a very powerful tool. It will carry you through this difficult time."

I closed my eyes and nodded several times. Placing my hand over my heart, I met his eyes. "Thank you."

"Don't mention it. Now, where can I take you? Back to the mansion?"

"No." I fidgeted and gave him a darting glance. "May I stay at your home tonight?"

He didn't even hesitate. "Of course." He rose to his feet and offered me his hand. "Come."

I smiled and took his hand. He pulled me to my feet, wrapping his arm about my waist, and escorted me out of the club. The cool night wind embraced my skin like a long-lost lover. I moaned and let my body sag against Ptah.

"Are you all right?"

I nodded. "Just relishing the night breeze."

He took it into his lungs. "It is a rather lovely night. Perfect for a quick jaunt through the air." Gripping my waist a little tighter, he whispered, "Hold on."

As we sailed through the air, he clutched at me like a mother would a fallen baby bird. The shimmering stars whizzed past, twirling against the midnight-blue sky. I couldn't tell if the illusion was caused by the speed at which we traveled or my drunken state. Either way, I had to hide my face inside his jacket to lessen the dizziness.

"We're almost there," he whispered in my ear.

I became less restless as our speed slowed and we descended toward the ground. Gliding in, we landed softly upon the ring-shaped driveway of his beachfront property. He steadied me before releasing me and making his way to the front door, and I staggered behind.

Natural stone landscaping and recessed copper lighting surrounded the estate. The circular three-story mansion sat by the edge of the ocean's cliff. The massive west wall was nearly all glass windows, and each stared straight out into the sea. The east wall was built into the mountainside, offering only a view of solid rock.

Ptah had purchased the vacant lot in Castle Beach three years ago, personally designing every square foot, and even performing a hands-on role in the construction. This meant he could boast to everyone, something he loved to do, that he'd created his home with his own bare hands. Having him as a close neighbor became a godsend to me. Many a late night I'd wandered onto his doorstep, drunk of course, seeking solitude and shelter from the sun, and sometimes from Philippe. Ptah provided both, without lecture or scowl—just an open door and a warm smile—and tonight was no different.

Unlocking the oversized slate door, he pushed it open and led me inside. Like my mother, he didn't believe in color. Modern black-and-white furniture with clean lines occupied every room in his home. Even the abstract paintings and bizarre sculptures were of the same limited palette.

He settled me into the snake-shaped leather sofa facing the window and held up a finger. "Be back in a minute with a warm mug of blood."

Reclining into the cushions, my gaze fell outside the window and centered on the dead-calm sea. Its stillness made the scene resemble a watercolor painting. A subtle swell rippled over the water, breaking the illusion—or was it a trick of drunken eyes?

Ptah returned, and the fragrant scent of salty blood perfumed the air, making my mouth water. Handing me the mug, he said, "Drink."

Wrapping both hands around the comfortingly warm mug, I inhaled deeply. Taking a sip while eyeing him over the rim, I asked, "How is it you seem to have a never-ending supply of blood?"

He winked at me. "Gifts from my fans. Humans adore me, and I've never been one to turn down a gift, especially when it's blood."

How his so-called fans provided blood he didn't let on, and I didn't know how to press for details. I let out a, "Huh," and then returned my focus to the sea. "I love it here, sitting on your sofa, staring at the ocean, drinking warm blood. Sometimes it's the only time I feel at peace."

He sat next to me and placed his hand on my knee. "You know I never meddle in your life, but I must say something. Don't let doubt destroy you. Hold onto your memories of Amon's love for you. It would pain him to see you so distraught."

I heaved a sigh and allowed my shoulders to sag. "I wish it were that simple."

"Is the friction between you and Philippe adding to your uncertainty?" He shook his head. "I don't see why you stay with him. It's quite clear Amon has claimed your heart."

I set the mug on the chrome coffee table, busying my hands over my face and through my hair. "I don't know. This whole binding business has changed everything. One minute I'm ready to pack my things, and the next I can't bear to leave." I glanced at Ptah. "Philippe and I took vows, for better or worse." I barked out a laugh. "This is definitely for the worst."

He pursed his lips. "Philippe has not been changed by the binding ritual. Only his façade has ended."

I gave a confused shake of my head. "What?"

"All these years, Philippe had to be someone else, someone you loved—who wasn't him." His brows came together, and he lowered his head to match my eye level. "He impersonated Amon. Attempting to take on his personality traits, Philippe pulled the wool over your eyes."

I tightened my jaw and looked away. Ptah was right, but I didn't want to listen. I wanted to believe Philippe wouldn't deceive me like that. An unnatural chill crept over my flesh. I shivered and rubbed my hands over my arms. My mind rushed back to that cold winter night so long ago when we'd first met. Philippe had stood before me, claiming to be the vampire I loved, and I eagerly believed him. I sagged into the sofa even further. "I know you're right."

Leaning in and looking me dead in the eyes, he insisted, "I am right. Only when he came face to face with Amon did he confess the truth. With Amon back in the picture, the real Philippe has slowly begun to resurface."

My hands fell to my sides, and I sat very quietly, staring straight ahead. I didn't want to hear anymore.

"Beth, are you okay?" he asked, breaking the silence.

I cupped my chin in the palm of my hand and closed my eyes. "Amon needs to come back so we can all move on with our lives, whichever direction that is."

"We need to create a diversion. Get your mind off your troubles and focus on something else, something fun." He snapped his fingers. "I've got it. A party."

I opened my eyes and rolled them at his words. "A party...really? I don't see how that could possibly improve my situation."

He rose from the sofa and stood with his arms crossed. He grinned, and his eyes twinkled. "Not just any party; a grand, fourteenth-century gala of kings and queens."

I waved a hand in the air dismissively. "Well, Philippe will love that. Our whole bedroom is decked out in pieces from that era."

"Forget about Philippe for a second." He stood tall, bowed, and then held out his hand. "My lady, may I have this dance?"

I batted my eyelashes, offering my hand. "Why yes, my lord."

Pulling me to my feet, he smiled as he slipped an arm about my waist, holding up my hand in fine waltzing form. I gazed into his almond-colored eyes and smiled. As our fingers locked, he set us in motion, twirling us about the room and humming a lovely melody into my ear.

I let out a giggle, and then another, and another, which eventually transformed into raucous laughter. By the time we slowed, I was gasping for air.

"See, you can have fun."

I fell back onto the couch, curling my legs beneath me. "Point taken. So when do you plan to hold this gala?"

"I...I don't know." He scooped his cell phone off the coffee table. "I'll call Brit. She handles all the events for my PR firm."

I held up my arm, tapping my watch. "It's five-thirty in the morning."

He dismissed me with a wave of his hand. "She's always up at the crack of dawn. Probably already in the office." He flashed a goofy grin. "I'll admit that I'm quite taken with her."

"*You* fell for a human?"

He frowned and then shrugged his shoulders weakly. "It appears so."

"Tell me about her. What's she like?"

The goofy grin expanded. "She's a chatterbox. Never shuts up but is extremely intelligent." He held his hand at a height just below his shoulder. "She's about yea high, with these gorgeous big blue eyes that I could stare into for all eternity."

I winked at him. "You really are taken with her. Have you asked her out?"

He jerked his head back and forth, panic stealing into his eyes. "I've formed the words on my tongue...but so far, always chicken out."

I shook my head at him. "Why? You're smart, successful, handsome, and kind. She'd be crazy to say no."

He tapped his cell phone against his leg. "Perhaps...but let's tackle one problem at a time. Yours first, then mine." He touched the face of his phone, brought it to his ear, and then waited. Breaking into a brisk jaunt around the sofa, he finally spoke. "Brit, it's Ptah. Listen...I need your help planning an event. Can you swing by my house this evening around six?" He bobbed his head and smiled. "Great. See you then." He came to a stop in front of me, dropping the phone and pointing a finger at me. "Don't start. I can see the matchmaker wheels turning in your head."

Clasping my hands around my knee, I said, "But I've got a perfect plan."

He folded his arms. "I'm listening."

"You could invite her to the gala. Ask her to come as your queen. Call it a reward for all her hard planning."

The corner of his mouth twitched and then spread into a crooked grin. "That does sound brilliant." He bent and kissed the top of my head.

"But for now, let's get some sleep." He tilted his head toward the stairs. "As always, you're welcome to one of the bedrooms."

Settling back into the cushions, I sighed and said, "I'm good right here with my mug of blood and view of the ocean."

"Good thing I had the contractor install protected films on all the windows." He grabbed an afghan off a chair and covered me, even tucking me in. "Good night."

"Good night."

CHAPTER 2

The rousing aroma of blood exploded inside my head, snapping me out of my slumbering state. Wide awake, I swung my legs over the side of the sofa to find a fresh mug of blood on the coffee table. A folded sheet of paper tucked under its edge caught my eye. I flipped it open to find the words *drink me* staring back from the page. I smirked. Would he start calling me Alice now, too? I took a generous swallow of the satisfying, metallic liquid.

Distant laughter sounded in my left ear. The murmur of voices came from inside Ptah's game room. Leaning forward, I eavesdropped on their conversation. An unfamiliar female chatted on about the gala, monopolizing the discussion while Ptah squeezed in a word here and there. Had to be Brit; how could I pass up the chance to meet the mysterious human who'd captivated Ptah's heart? Absolutely, I could not. I raced over to the game room, coming to a dead stop in the doorway. Then I glided inside, nonchalantly making my entrance.

Ptah approached me, draping his arm over my shoulder. "Brit, this is Beth, a dear friend of mine. Beth, this is Brit, my right hand and PR guru."

The slim girl with short, jet-black hair and high cheekbones crossed the floor and extended her hand. "Nice to meet you."

I took her hand. "And you."

"I was just telling Ptah this room would be perfect for the gala." She peeked at us over her shoulder. "Of course, we'd have to remove the furniture, especially the pool table."

"I agree," Ptah blurted out.

She shifted toward the glass doors, throwing them open and stepping out onto the patio. "This could become the fencing arena where kings once dueled to the death." She added, "Figuratively, of course."

Ptah followed her around, nodding at everything she said. I suppressed a giggle. "Yes, brilliant," he said. "Love it." He turned to me. "Wouldn't you agree, Beth?"

If she suggested flying monkeys serving blood to his guests, he'd agree. I wasn't about to intrude on his bliss. "Most definitely."

She turned in a slow circle, her baby blues doubling in size. She faced Ptah and clasped her hands together in excitement. "What fun would it be if it were a masked gala?"

I pointed a finger at her, elated. "Fabulous! Love the idea of masked kings and queens." I looked to Ptah. "Let's do it?"

He slapped his thigh. "Done."

"Let's choose an area for food," she rattled off, stepping back inside and veering toward the entryway. "We'll place high-backed thrones along the walls, and the left wall is perfect for an extra-long table filled with food." She tilted her head. "And maybe in that corner, we can stand a couple of suits of armor."

"I can provide those," I said, throwing up my hand. Philippe wouldn't mind. Hell, he'd probably be proud to display the silly things.

"Very good." She turned to Ptah and frowned. "Most guests will be immortal, which creates a challenge for the menu." She tapped a finger against her chin, staring at Ptah. "Wine is a given, but as for cuisine, I'm stumped."

Ptah wasn't thinking of food. He straightened his shirt, cleared his throat, and neared her. Gazing into her eyes, he asked, "Brit, will you join me at the gala as my queen? I...I mean, it could be—"

Her cheeks flushed rosy red, a girlish smile playing across her lips as she cut his stammering off. "Yes, I would like that very much."

His expression reminded me of a schoolboy with his first crush. My cue to leave. I backed soundlessly toward the front door, slipping out of the house. A light wind carried the salty fragrance of the ocean to me. The urge to rush to the seashore nearly overpowered me, but I turned in the opposite direction instead, heading home for a shower and a change of clothes.

Shoulders back and a spring in my step, I began to hum, envisioning the flurry of kings and queens gliding across a dance floor. Ptah was right. Creating a distraction took the edge off the loneliness imprisoning my heart, diminishing the itch to drown my sorrows in wine.

I felt as close to normal as I could get with Amon somewhere out in the world I had no knowledge of. I couldn't change the situation, but I could change my approach to it. Take one day at a time. Definitely less daunting than facing the big picture. "Yes, I like it," I said aloud, solidifying my resolve.

I soon reached our driveway. I swung my arms and skipped all the way to the front door. When I entered the foyer, my gaze fell upon Philippe sitting on the bottom stair, awaiting my return. His eyes sparkled as they fell on me. Instantly he was on his feet. Holding out his hand, he said, "Come, I have something to show you."

Taking his hand, my brow wrinkling, I asked, "What's this about?"

"You'll see." He led me up the staircase and down the hallway, just past our room to an open doorway. He ushered me inside. "Wait here."

As I waited, I announced Ptah's plans. "Ptah mentioned hosting a kings and queens' gala. I offered up your suits of armor as part of the décor. I hope you don't mind."

"Fine," he called out, apparently uninterested or perhaps preoccupied in his big reveal.

A rectangular table cluttered with paint and brushes sat in the center of the room. Off to its right a rather large canvas, covered by a sheet, rested on an easel.

"You paint?" My eyes fell over the length of the table.

He smiled. "Now and then."

Turning in a circle, I scanned the room. "How is it possible to live with someone for over five years and never know all of their talents?"

He waved my question away. "Never mind that." Entwining our fingers, he led me to the covered canvas. "I've been working on this piece for a few days. At first I wasn't pleased with it. There was something missing, an attribute I couldn't capture, but then it came to me." Gripping the edge of the cloth, he tugged it away. "I've created a masterpiece."

The cloth fell to the floor, revealing a striking portrait of me, painted in shades of cream, gold, and brown. He'd painted me with my gaze cast downward as if I felt heartbroken, yet my face contained a hint of happiness. The emotion captured was love.

I gasped and grabbed his arm. Tears rose in my eyes. The Philippe I once knew was capable of such a kind gesture. Was the painting his way of putting our relationship back together and expressing his love? Perhaps I'd been wrong to judge, to have been at odds with him—and I'd called him an Amon imposter. I stepped closer, running a finger over the layers of paint.

His gaze followed me. "You have tears in your eyes. Do you love it or hate it?"

A rush of breath escaped my lungs, and I spread my hand over my heart. "I love it." I shook my head and softly whispered, "It's beautiful." I reached for his hand. "Thank you. Where should we hang it?"

He blinked and looked away, then back to me. "Oh, no, I'm sorry. This isn't...I didn't mean for you to...Caleb asked me to create something for his gallery opening. The painting is for him."

I lowered my head, pressing my lips in a hard line. Slowly I raised my eyes to meet his. "Silly me," I said, raising my voice. "I thought this came from your heart, a token of your affection or an expression of love. I should have known better." Turning my back on him, I rushed from the room and into the hallway.

He ran after me, catching my arm and spinning me around. "If you want the painting, I'll give it to you. I can create something else for Caleb."

I pushed his hand away and shook my head. "You're missing the point. I thought it was a gift. Giving it to me now is meaningless." Again, I left him, taking large strides toward our bedroom.

He rushed in front of me, halting my progress. "Wait, please. I didn't stop to think, and I never meant to hurt you." He blew out a sigh and offered me a half smile. "I showed the painting to you because I wanted you to see how beautiful I think you are. By displaying it in the gallery, the world will know how I feel." He narrowed the gap between us and cupped my face in his hands. "I love you so much I can't see straight. I want to make you happy. I fear I rarely do anymore." He dropped his hands and took a step back, but his eyes never left mine. "You're slipping away from me. Don't, please."

I could feel my pulse quickening in my throat. My hands trembled at my sides. "I don't know what I feel anymore," I answered softly.

One eyebrow twitched, and he swallowed hard. "Don't give up on me. I'll try harder." His grin widened. "Come with me to Caleb's gallery. I have to drop off the painting tonight. Afterward, we can take a walk on the beach, maybe stop somewhere for a glass of wine."

Looking into his gray-blue eyes was like looking into the past. The Philippe I once loved stood in front of me, wearing his heart on his sleeve. How could I say no? "Yes, I'll come with you. Just give me ten minutes. I need a quick shower and a change of clothes."

"Of course. I'll wrap the painting and have Jon Paul pull the car around." He kissed my cheek. "See you soon."

Continuing to our room at a brisk pace, I ran my hands through my hair and bit my lip. Was I making the right decision in joining him and behaving as if things could be set right? Maybe they could be. Didn't I owe him that chance? I was still his wife after all, regardless of what I felt for Amon. Ptah's words crept into my head. He was right. I needed to make a decision and choose. I couldn't have them both, but I wanted them both.

After freshening up, I headed downstairs, strolled through the foyer, and out the front door. Philippe stood by the rear of the BMW watching Jon Paul lower the painting into the trunk. As I neared them, Jon Paul hurried around the side of the car to open the door for me. Climbing inside, I scooted to the opposite side. Philippe followed suit, sitting a good foot away from me. Jon Paul shut the door, hopped into the driver's seat, and started the engine. Hugging the circular drive, he coasted down the driveway away from the house and then turned onto the street, picking up speed.

Inching a bit closer to me, Philippe tucked a strand of my hair behind my ear and said, "You're so beautiful. I know I've been a jerk. I've driven a wedge between us, but you have to understand how hard this is for me."

I snapped my head in his direction, knitting my brows together. "And it's not for me?"

He held up his hand in a placating gesture. "I'm not saying that." He fell silent and stared at me for several minutes before continuing. "I know you love Amon. I know you love him more than me."

I opened my mouth, but no words came out. It was true, but not why he thought. With each beat of my heart, the binding ritual strengthened my love for Amon. It wasn't Philippe who drove the wedge; it was the damned binding ritual.

"I never should have pretended to be the vampire you loved." He lowered his gaze and shifted away from me. "I wanted to confess, but my selfish needs outweighed my guilt." His eyes locked on mine. "And we were so happy...until Amon showed up."

He kept swallowing and fidgeting with the buttons on his shirt. A part of me wanted to comfort him, but I could only sit very still, staring at him.

He ran his hand over his mouth. "I'm not saying he's to blame. This is my fault. I wish I could go back in time and do everything all over again."

"I wish that too," I told him.

He faced me, searching my eyes with his own. "I'd let you fall in love with me, the real me. No lies, no secrets."

I slumped against my seat and heaved a sigh. "But we can't go back, Philippe, only forward."

He took my hand and gave it a squeeze. "That's why I'm asking you not to give up on me. Please, Beth."

I drew my shoulders in and grabbed onto my elbows, pulling them in close. How could I respond to him? I didn't have an answer. I craved Amon's love, but when I looked at Philippe, a twinge gripped my heart. The strength of the emotion echoed through my heart. Part of my soul still belonged to Philippe. I couldn't let him go; although, at the same time, I wanted to run far away from him and never look back.

The car slowed, sidling up to the curb and coming to a complete stop. Jon Paul's footsteps grew louder as he reached my door and opened it. Taking Jon Paul's hand, I stepped from the car onto the sidewalk facing Caleb's gallery. He had named it *The Gallery*. It wasn't the most original, but the way the large, gray, italicized letters flowed across the glass window was simply beautiful and timeless. I loved it.

Jon Paul opened the trunk so Philippe could remove the painting. "We shouldn't be long, Jon Paul. Just dropping this off. Afterward, we'll take a drive by the beach."

Jon Paul nodded. "Very well, Mr. Delon. Let me get the front door for you." He jogged up to the gallery door and held it open. After we crossed the threshold, Jon Paul went back to stand by the car, folding his arms behind his back.

The narrow room contained several abstract pieces on display, scattered across the hardwood floor. Paintings of various sizes dotted the clean, white walls. The bizarre pieces with odd-colored palettes, wild brush strokes, and distorted shapes were not my cup of tea.

"Has the sky finally fallen? Beth has graced us with her presence!" Caleb projected his voice across the room. He plastered a sneer on his face, radiating superiority, before moving closer to us. "To what do I owe the pleasure?"

I rolled my eyes. Same old Caleb.

Philippe stepped in front of me, holding out the painting. In a curt tone, he said, "Put a sock in it, Caleb."

Caleb shrugged his shoulders and eyed Philippe with feigned innocence. "What?"

"You know exactly what," Philippe told him, shaking his head. "Now, where do you want the painting?"

Ignoring his question for the moment, Caleb came to kiss me on my cheek. "It's good to see you."

I touched his arm and mustered up what I hoped was a charming smile. "And you."

Caleb left my side to retrieve the canvas by its edges, setting the painting on the floor. After pulling away the brown paper wrapping, Caleb took a large step back to assess the painting, his hands on his hips. He gave a slow, disbelieving shake of his head and then turned to face Philippe and me. A huge smile graced his lips as he clapped his hands. "Bravo! Absolutely superb!" He glanced over his shoulder at the painting and then turned back to me. "It's like looking at Beth in the flesh." He turned and drank in the painting again, shaking his head. "I love it."

Philippe bowed his head. "Thank you." He glanced at me. "It's close to my heart."

I clamped my lips together. *Really? Is that why you're handing it over to Caleb, because it's so special? Why we argued over how you presented it to me? Unbelievable.* I forced a smile and kept my mouth shut.

Caleb carried it to the middle of the room, facing a blank wall. "This is the perfect spot for it. Philippe, grab a corner and help me center it on the hook."

Philippe strutted over to Caleb like a proud lion, taking up the left side. Together they hoisted the canvas upward and onto the hook. Stepping back, they cocked their heads in unison.

"A little to the right," Caleb said, inching the likeness of me just a hair in that direction. He released the canvas, giving it the once-over. With a firm nod, he said, "Spot on." He looked back at me. "Beth, do you agree?"

I gave him a thumbs up and then shoved my hands into my pants pockets. Ultimately, it would hang on some stranger's wall. What did I care whether it was straight or crooked?

Philippe returned to my side and slipped his arm around my waist. "Well, we're off. Gonna take a walk on the beach."

Caleb waved us away. "Enjoy."

We exited The Gallery, and Jon Paul was waiting. Standing tall, he took a large sideways step and clasped the door handle, opening it for us. "To the beach, Mr. Delon?"

"Sea Cliff has amazing waves this time of year," Philippe said, helping me into the car and then climbing in after me. He settled next to me and took my hand. "That's our destination."

"Of course, sir," Jon Paul answered, pushing the door shut.

Sea Cliff was a stone's throw from The Gallery, so close we could have walked. Why Philippe had asked Jon Paul to drive us there escaped me. Was it an intentional excuse to snuggle next to me, like two teenagers in the backseat of a car? I shook my head, rejecting the idea. The crazy-romantic phase of our relationship had ended shortly after Amon disappeared; that, combined with the binding ritual, was to blame. Each year a piece of my heart swayed toward Amon. It seemed I lived, breathed, and dreamed Amon. Whoever said, "Absence makes the heart grow fonder," they weren't kidding.

Jon Paul pulled away from the curb, navigating a quick U-turn and heading toward Sea Cliff.

"You're awfully quiet," Philippe said, brushing his lips against my ear.

I fixed my gaze straight ahead. If I turned, he'd kiss me on my lips. At the moment, the ones I wished to touch mine weren't his. Shrugging my shoulders, I said, "Not much to say."

"Then I'll do all the talking. I know you didn't really want to come out with me, so thank you for giving me tonight and for trying."

I squeezed his hand, and in a gentle tone I reassured him. "Don't be silly. I wanted to come with you. This isn't easy for either one of us."

"Please look at me." His tone was on the verge of begging.

My cheeks burned. How could I not? I was still his wife. Slowly, I turned to face him.

He gave me a droopy half-smile and then brushed the back of his hand down my cheek. "I love you, Beth, and I'm sorry. Sorry for everything I've done wrong."

My stomach quivered, and I leaned away from him. After five years, the sudden desire to make things right spilled out of his mouth? Could I give him hope knowing someday Amon would return to me? What then? Only time held that answer, and possibly Isis, Hathor, and Osiris. "I—I don't know what to say."

He pressed a finger to my lips. "You don't have to say anything. You need time, time to trust me again. Just give me some time. That's all I ask."

It was painfully obvious he was competing for my heart. The words flowed from my mouth as if I had no control over them. "Of course, I will."

His mouth fell open in shock before the smile returned to his face. He reached to pull me close, squeezing tight as if he'd never let me go.

Jon Paul stopped the car and then freed us from the back seat. "Should I wait, Mr. Delon?"

Philippe gave him a firm nod. "We'll be back within the hour."

"Very well, sir." Jon Paul settled behind the driver's seat with a newspaper.

Philippe took my arm, ushering me away from the car and onto the ocean's border of cool, wet sand. A handful of stars dotted the pitch-black sky, and salt was carried on the crisp breeze. Waves crashed at our feet as we strolled along the shoreline.

Several paces into our stride, loud, animated voices off in the distance rang in my vampire ears. About a football field away were eight, perhaps ten, drunken humans slurring their words and laughing loudly around a fire pit. Their thumping heartbeats collided, slamming together like one massive jackhammer, jarring me to my core.

Philippe pulled me closer and whispered into my ear, "I feel like having a midnight snack. How about you?"

I glanced toward the ignorantly blissful humans, skimming their thoughts. Not one wished for death. I faced Philippe.

A devilish grin lay upon his lips. "They won't even know what hit them."

I drew my eyebrows together, mustering up a harsh expression of disapproval. "None of those people want to die."

His grin quickly faded as he stared at me blankly.

I threw my words at him. "Your victims want death, remember? That's why you choose them, or at least that's what you want everyone to believe." I jutted out my hand, pointing at the humans. "No one over there holds a welcoming thought for death."

He cleared his throat. "You're right. They don't."

I didn't say anything else, just glared at him.

Staring down at his feet, he said, "I made that up years ago when we first met and you were still human." He lifted his head and looked directly into my eyes. "Back then, you wanted to watch me feed. I couldn't have you thinking I was a monster, so I told you my victims wanted death. I guess I just kept up the charade."

The veins at my temples throbbed, drowning out the repetitive thump of the human heartbeats in the distance. More lies. Was he hiding something deeper? Had he been keeping secrets from me? Or was there something more to him than I had ever realized? Curling my fingers into a ball of exasperation, I exploded. "Will your lies never end?"

He came to me, clasping my hands, his words rushing from his lips. "I'm being honest now. Please, you must believe me."

I let go of him and stepped backward, widening the space between us. "How can I trust anything you say? Was anything true or real?"

"Yes, of course."

I challenged him by dredging up his past. "Were you really a knight? Did your best friend betray you? Did Caleb save you from death and turn you?"

Splaying his hand across his heart, he poured conviction into his voice. "Yes, every word."

I threw another tale he'd once told me at him. "What about Dana and his daughter? Lies or truth?"

He threw his hands up. "All truth; I swear it."

I let out a theatrical groan before raising my voice. "Don't make me keep guessing. If there is anything, anything at all, you're still hiding, out with it."

He pinned his arms against his stomach, released what appeared to be a painful breath, and then confessed, "I was never going to tell you how I'd deceived you. Then Amon showed up and forced my hand. Caleb's instruction on how you could hide your past from me was a perfect cover. I used it to protect myself."

A bone-deep cold overtook me, and every muscle inside my limbs went rigid. When I could move again, I turned my back on him and marched toward the car. I barked out, "Take me home."

He caught up to me, hovering by my side and matching my stride. Shoving his hands into his pockets, he kept his eyes on the path, not speaking a word. Maybe he sensed we had nothing to talk about. The silence calmed me. My heartbeat slowed, finding its normal rhythm; although, at the moment, I wanted to be anywhere but by his side. The faster Jon Paul got us home, the better. I bolted straight for the car.

Jon Paul zipped out of the car to swing open my door seconds before I arrived. After noting my expression, he avoided eye contact as I slid into the back seat. Philippe climbed in after me, sticking close to the door and as far from me as possible.

Jon Paul's voice seemed strained when he asked, "Where to, Mr. Delon?"

"Home," Philippe answered in a clipped tone.

"Very well," Jon Paul said, closing us in.

As we pulled onto the road Philippe sank low in his seat, staring out the window. Cupping my chin in the palm of my hand, I did the same, focusing on the broken white lines rushing beside us on the pavement below. Why did I stay? For the torture? To suffer? Was my life nothing more than relentless disappointment and frustration? *Certainly not.* One of us had to let go, but I couldn't. Whether or not I wanted to admit it, Philippe gave me inner strength. I had two choices: stay or go. I'd surrendered to the lesser of two evils and chosen to stay.

Not one word was spoken between us the entire ride home. As soon as Jon Paul shifted into park, I blasted from the car, not waiting to have my door opened. Philippe was right on my heels. Pushing open the front door, I stormed inside the house, smashing into Betty and knocking her to the floor.

Betty let out a sharp cry of pain.

"Beth!" Philippe snapped.

After scooping her up and setting her gently on her feet, I apologized. "Betty, I'm so sorry. Forgive me."

She brushed off her clothes and took a couple of deep breaths. "I'm okay."

Philippe looked her up and down, acquiring confirmation. "You're sure?"

She shooed him away. "Yes, yes, I'm fine." She placed her hands on her hips. "But I can't say the same for the two of you, now can I?"

She was absolutely right. Shame forced my head down, and I glanced at Philippe to find it had done the same to him. Gripping the edges of my jacket, I pulled it closed and waited to be scolded like a naughty child.

She stood tall, her gaze acidic. "I haven't a clue what's happened between the two of you, and, frankly, it's none of my business, but since I love you both like family, I can't just stand by and watch you destroy each other this way." She relaxed slightly, her hands dropping to her sides. "Talk to each other. Work it out. You loved each other once. Remember that." She gave a curt nod and then hurried away, letting her statement sink in.

As her footsteps grew faint, even with vampire hearing, I turned toward the staircase, paying no heed to her words.

"Beth," Philippe's tone was pitiful, injured.

I froze in my tracks but didn't turn to face him. "What?"

"Forgive me, please."

If I turn around, I'll give in. Planting a foot firmly on the bottom stair, I said only, "Good night, Philippe," before jogging up the staircase.

CHAPTER 3

The next few nights I avoided Philippe, taking refuge instead inside Bloodthirst. A smorgasbord of human blood wandered by, right at my fingertips. Puncturing neck after neck, sweet nectar flowed steadily into my eager mouth. I drank to my heart's content, getting high on their life's essence, but most importantly, I let them live.

Tingling with warm human blood, I strolled through the flock of smitten mortals. Craving a glass of red wine to wash down all the blood, I made my way to the bar, occasionally acknowledging an admirer with a slight nod.

Inches from the sanctuary of the counter, a slender hand slipped around my arm, pulling me aside. Margarete's voice filled my ear. "I've been watching you."

Facing her, I answered, "I'm assuming there's a reason behind that?"

Her violet-colored eyes grew wide, but she never blinked. Leaning closer, she continued. "You're like a clever little bee collecting pollen; well, pollen in this case being blood."

I replied only with a smirk.

"What are you up to?"

I laughed. "Nothing. I just don't want to kill anymore."

She pressed her lips into a fine line. "We have to kill."

I locked my eyes on hers. "No...we...don't."

Gripping at my sleeve, she yanked me forward, approaching a fair-haired young male. "You," she barked. "Come."

He rushed to her side, rubbed his hands together, and blurted out, "Finally."

"Stay," she said, stretching out her arm and holding up her hand an inch from his face.

I sighed heavily. "He's not a dog, Margarete."

She tossed her hair over her shoulder, dismissing me with a wave of her hand. "*He* is not my concern. Now, how do I feed without killing? Show me."

I stepped in front of him, blocking her access. "It's not easy. I can't just show you. You'll have to do it on your own."

"Fine. Tell me then."

I leveled my gaze and said nothing, letting the tension build between us.

"Well?" she asked, tapping her foot in impatience.

"You count. Each human gets sixty seconds. Release them and move on to the next." I spread my arms and smiled sarcastically "It's that simple."

Her eyes narrowed, focusing on me, and then she darted toward the human. Latching onto him, she sank her fangs deep into his jugular. He leaned into her, stroking the small of her back. She let out a soft cry, her eyes rolling up to show the whites. They clung to each other as if sharing a fervent kiss. She held no thought of letting him go. I tugged aggressively at her arm. She swatted at me as if I were a fly.

Seizing a handful of her hair, I jerked her head backward, screaming, "Margarete, stop!"

She hissed and snarled, tightening her grip. He slumped forward in her arms, limp like a doll.

The hair lifted on the nape of my neck. What a fool I'd been to trust her. I crushed her chin between my fingers, twisting her head around, forcing her to look at him. "You're killing him."

Her eyes bulged and she bolted backward, dropping him. He staggered a step or two, gave his head a good shake, and then touched the base of his neck. His eyes popped wide as he gazed down at his blood-stained fingertips.

I pushed him away. "Go, you fool."

He stumbled off, clutching at his throat and murmuring under his breath, "I wanted more."

"What a rush," Margarete whispered into my ear. "I must try again."

I shoved her against the wall and held her there. "Are you kidding me? No way in hell."

"I can do this," she said with conviction.

"If I hadn't stopped you, you would have killed him."

She shrugged halfheartedly. "He's a lab rat. The club's full of them."

"Shut up. Just shut up." I turned my back to her.

"Wait," she said, lightly touching my shoulder. "I'm not like you, Beth. I'm not compassionate." She stepped in front of me and tucked her hands behind her elbows. "I don't know how to be."

"It's not something you know. It's something you feel."

Her lips pressed together in a thin line. "Have a drink with me. Let me tell you a story."

My ears perked up. I was a sucker for a good story. "Why not?" I said, throwing my hands in the air.

She held up her hand, flagging the bartender. His dark-brown eyes lit up as he gazed upon her. Was he an admirer? Maybe a lover?

"Two glasses of Merlot," she demanded, and then blew him a kiss.

He winked at her, poured the wine, and set the glasses on the counter. "On the house, Margarete."

She flashed a flirty smile, scooped up both glasses, and turned away. Glancing over her shoulder, she said, "Why, thank you, Marco."

"Who's Marco?" I whispered into her ear.

Handing me a glass, she answered, "No one." With her free hand, she led me by the arm to a booth tucked away in a private corner of the club. She jerked her head to the right. "Sit."

I placed my glass down but didn't budge an inch.

In a softer tone, she tried again. "Please, sit."

I scooted into the seat to sit opposite her, plopping my elbows down on the table and resting my head in my hands. "I'm all ears."

She took a sip of her wine and closed her eyes. "I was kidnapped by hunters when I was only seventeen. The year was 1897." She opened her eyes and latched onto mine.

"You mean vampire hunters?"

She let out a deep sigh. "Yes. I grew up in London...then and now, the command center for hunters. They needed a test subject, and I wouldn't be missed by anyone. You see, I was an outcast, even within my own family."

The way she let *test subject* roll off her tongue like it meant nothing at all tore at my gut, but for the life of me, I couldn't grasp why a vampire hunter would kidnap Margarete.

"I'm a medium...a spirit vessel, so to speak," she answered, as if she'd read my mind, and knowing Margarete, she probably had. "Voices are constantly rambling on inside my head. When I was younger, I couldn't turn them off." Her gaze shifted across the table in a discreet manner. "I would have conversations with them, yelling at them in public. A costly mistake on my part. People assumed I was talking to myself. Called me crazy. The townspeople wanted nothing to do with me and kept their distance."

I grabbed my wine and took a generous swallow. *Spirits inside your head? I couldn't handle that.* "Are you saying hunters took you because of your connection to the other side?"

She fixed on something in the distance, before slowly returning to meet my eyes. "No. Like I said, they needed a subject, and I was an easy target. No one would come looking for a crazy person."

I sat back and stared at her. Not a single enlightening emotion played in her eyes, almost as if she were speaking of someone other than herself.

"After a sleepless night of spirit jabber, I went for a walk to clear my head. It was early...still dark out. They came out of nowhere, threw a bag over my head, and pressed a damp handkerchief with a horrid stench over my mouth. I don't remember blacking out, but I must have. I awoke in a cell-like room on a cold, hard cot."

I inched closer to her, close enough to grab hold of her hand in a gesture of reassurance.

She smirked and then gently untangled my hand from her own. "It was a hundred and eighteen years ago, Beth. You don't have to comfort me."

I ignored her and reclaimed her hand. "Go on."

She let out a huff but didn't push me away. "Not long after I re-gained consciousness, several men came into my cell, strong-arming a young man and thrusting him in my direction. A tall man with a thick beard pointed at me and ordered, "Turn her."

"The man they forced on you was a vampire," I blurted out.

She nodded before quickly continuing. "But he refused, vehemently shaking his head from side to side. The tall man sneered and pulled a gun from inside his coat. 'Then she dies,' he stated with dead calm. I jumped to my feet screaming bloody murder, to no avail. No one could hear my screams."

I shrugged in disbelief. "It doesn't make sense. Why would they threaten him with your life? Did you know this vampire?"

She took a long pause before responding. "I'd never seen him before in my life." A radiant glow infused her cheeks. "Though now, I know him very well." She nodded toward the stage. "Each night he lays out the rules of the club."

I dropped her hand, my finger jutting toward the stage. "The host, he turned you?"

In a quiet voice, she said, "His name is Willard...and it wasn't that simple."

"Okay, I'll bite. What happened?"

Continuing in the same unruffled tone, she told me the rest. "The man stepped closer, jamming the barrel of the gun against the side of my temple. I crawled inside myself, keeping very still. I didn't even blink. My eyes were glued to the vampire.

"The vampire began to weep. He mumbled a word that could have been *monsters* and then slowly inched over to me. The man's lips spread into a smug grin. He lowered his gun and ordered, 'Do it.'

"The vampire cupped my face in his hands. 'I'm sorry,' he whispered in a genuinely kind voice. It was all over in minutes. He drained the life from my body and then fed me his blood. I don't remember pain or death, only fervent pleasure engulfing my entire body...and finally, darkness. Again, I woke in the cell—alone, weak, feverish, and in a state of confusion. I was left this way for several days."

"Why? Why would they turn you and leave you like that?"

"The bastards wanted test subjects, like I said. I was their lab rat. They made me just to try and kill me."

I latched onto her arm with more force than I intended, but she didn't flinch. "What?!"

Her nostrils flared, and her eyes glossed over when she said, "The hunters performed experiments on me. Fed me garlic, rubbed it all over my skin, poured salt on me, staked my heart, deprived me of blood, let sunlight flood my cell, shot me with silver bullets, locked me inside a church, and splashed holy water on me. They tortured me day in and..." She stopped midstream for a moment to compose herself. "...day out. Thank God they were idiots. Never tried setting me on fire. If they had..."

I clenched my hands so tightly that my knuckles turned white. They *were* the monsters, torturing a seventeen-year-old girl like that. I embraced her, pulling her into a fierce hug. For a brief moment she trembled in my arms and then pulled away. After downing her wine, she sat up tall and proud, her customary vain expression resurfacing.

"I'm fine," she said, holding up her hand.

"You're sure?"

In answer, she jumped right back into the story. "I started marking off days in my cell with a piece of broken rock. On day ninety-five, I heard high-pitched shrieks through the walls. It sounded like pigs being slaughtered—hundreds of them—and the sound kept growing closer and closer, until it was right outside my cell. The door shook violently, the hinges popping apart. Whatever was out there was intent on coming in. I backed against the wall, doing my best to stay quiet."

"The screams, were they the hunters'?"

A satisfied smile made an appearance. "Yes. Willard killed every single one of them. He popped the last remaining hinge, grabbed onto my hand, and we fled. We didn't stop running, never staying in one place for very long, until we came here to Castle Beach and opened

Bloodthirst." She pulled her brows together and narrowed her gaze. "So now you see why I have no compassion for these humans."

I wished I could ease the pain of her past, but she had to realize not all humans were hunters. Most worshiped us, craved our companionship, and doted on us. Placing my hand over hers, I said, "These humans are not hunters. They come here driven by complete adoration. You must see that."

She rolled her eyes. "You're naïve. You see the good in everyone."

"And that's a bad thing?"

For a long moment she said nothing, just stared blankly. Finally, she gave me a warm smile. "No, that is not a bad thing."

****

Night after night I joined Margarete at Bloodthirst, training her to feed without taking life. It took a good solid week, with me detaching her from the necks of gullible, yet willing, victims, before she mastered the art.

Once she succeeded several times in controlling herself, she clapped her hands like a child and grabbed my arm. "We must celebrate by sharing a bottle of Merlot."

"Yes, we must," I responded. I wasn't about to argue with that logic.

Her eyes darted away from me and over the crowd. She dropped my arm and let out a loud groan. "What in the world is he doing here?"

Wondering about the source of her displeasure, I asked, "Who?" My mouth dropped open in disbelief, as I turned around. Philippe was heading straight for us.

"Your husband, that's who," she said with a huff. "He never comes here. Never." She crossed her arms in agitation. "Probably spying on us."

I was about to criticize and then stopped short. Margarete was partly right. It was uncharacteristic for Philippe to set foot inside Bloodthirst. He despised the place, but Margarete had to be way off on her theory. Spying was out of the question. Philippe respected my privacy. But then, why was he here?

He halted inches from me. His gray-blue eyes brightened, and a boyish smile adorned his face. "I've missed you."

Margarete heaved a dramatic sigh.

I shot her a look that silenced her and returned my attention to Philippe. "What are you doing here? You hate this place."

His gaze swept over the club. "True." Again he centered on me. "I figured to see you I had to come here. Can I bring you a glass of wine?"

I didn't take my eyes off him, moving closer into his personal space. He loathed Bloodthirst. Crossing its threshold just to be near me spoke volumes. The least I could do was have a drink with him. "I'd like that."

Margarete let out another groan.

Facing her, I reached for her hand and gave it a squeeze. "I'm so proud of you. Give me a rain check on that drink?"

She beamed, then as she raised her chin and threw her shoulders back. "I did do well, didn't I? Oh well, you know where to find me." I watched her vanish amidst the crowd.

Philippe placed his hand in the small of my back. "I see an open booth on the right. You take a seat, and I'll be right over with the wine."

"All right."

He leaned in, kissing my cheek. His lips lingered for a moment, and then he pulled away and headed toward the bar. For a brief moment I held him in my gaze, then turned and zigzagged between the patrons, making my way to the booth. I settled in the center, resting my elbows on the table, with no desire to be anywhere else.

Philippe emerged from the crowd carrying full glasses of dark-red wine in each hand. As he slid into the booth next to me, he handed me a glass and raised his. "A toast," he said. "To new beginnings."

I tightened my jaw and gave a halfhearted nod. I couldn't fully commit. Touching my glass to his, I offered up a compromise "To forgiveness."

His gaze held strong as he repeated, "To forgiveness."

We both took a generous swallow before setting our glasses on the table.

From his pocket he retrieved a gold envelope and pushed it my way. "Ptah hand-delivered this invitation yesterday."

I tore open the invite. "The honor of your presence is requested at the Masked Kings and Queens' Gala, Saturday, January 16." I blinked and read the date again. Jerking my head upright, I looked at Philippe. "Is he insane? That's this weekend! How can we find costumes that fast?"

Philippe chuckled before turning the invitation over. "That's what I thought too. But look: costumes, wigs, and masks will arrive the morning of the gala directly to our home." He winked at me. "And there's fencing."

I gave him a playful nudge. "Right up your alley, huh?"

Rubbing his hands together and kissing my cheek again, he said, "I love it. We're gonna have a blast!"

CHAPTER 4

The morning of the kings and queens' gala, I was pacing our foyer in my pajamas and bare feet. After every couple of passes, my eyes darted to the front door. Where the hell were our costumes?

Betty ambled in, carrying a stack of freshly folded linens. The delicate scent of lavender fragranced the air. She chuckled, stacked them on the foyer table, and placed her hands on her hips. "A watched pot never boils. Go back to bed. Get some sleep. I promise I'll wake you when the delivery arrives."

Twisting my wedding ring, I blurted out, "Sleep! I can't sleep. I just lie in bed and stare at the ceiling. I'm dying to know which queen I am."

"Very well, sit and wait." She picked up the sheets and started to walk away, then added, "Or in your case, wear a hole in the floor. I'll be upstairs making—"

The sudden chime of the doorbell slammed against my eardrums, drowning out her words. I lunged for the door, gripping the handle before I shrank back in a panic. Had I lost my mind? It was broad daylight. Sunshine was not my friend. Whirling around, I faced Betty. "The door...*please*, get the door."

"Hold your horses, dear, and give me an opportunity."

I didn't take my eyes off her as she once more set down the sheets and too casually approached the door and pulled it open.

"Yes?" she said.

A rather stocky man stood in our doorway. He gave her a curt nod and held up his clipboard. "Good morning, ma'am." His voice was as thick and deep as he was. "I have a delivery for Mr. and Mrs. Delon." He glanced down at his order and furrowed his brow. "I'm also to pick up two medieval suits of armor."

Betty stepped aside and swung the door wide open. "I will accept for them. Please, come inside." She pointed toward the stairs. "The armor is there."

With ease he wheeled a portable wardrobe closet through the doorway and into the foyer. The thing was massive, maybe six feet tall. "Where would you like it?" he asked, looking about, and then his peering came to a grinding halt as he focused on me. He regarded me up and down, and then a ridiculous grin materialized on his round face.

Betty eyed him, pursing her lips. In a crisp tone, she said, "Right there is fine."

He unloaded the closet and then turned his dolly toward the staircase, wheeling it over to the foot of the stairs. He collected Philippe's prize possessions one at a time, setting each gently on the platform. With one hand he steered the dolly in Betty's direction, stopped in front of her, and handed her a clipboard and pen. "Please sign here, ma'am," he said, his gaze wandering back to me.

Betty scribbled across the sheet of paper, passed the clipboard back to him, and then shooed him toward the door. When he was safely out on the porch, she said, "Thank you, and good day." After closing the door, she turned to me, shook her head, and mumbled, "Men."

I waved a dismissive hand in the air. "Forget him." I rushed to the wardrobe, sliding down the zipper with a good yank. "I feel like a kid on Christmas morning," I said, peeling back the front to reveal a black ruffled gown embroidered in gold. The tiny bodice seemed disproportionate to the flaring skirt. I giggled and glanced at Betty. "Three people could fit under there." Facing the dress, I shuffled back a step or two, touching my fingertips to my lips. "It's...gigantic but beautiful."

"Oh my!" Betty exclaimed. "It's absolutely stunning." She placed her hand on top of the fabric and ran it between her fingers. "And velvety soft." She barked out a laugh and plucked a bag off the wardrobe bar. "Get a load of this wig." Unzipping the bag and removing it caused her to laugh louder. "These blonde curls are piled at least a foot high. Whoever had this much hair?"

I eyed the wig. Was everything big back then? Why the exaggeration? "Who is this queen?" I asked, glancing through the wardrobe. "Is there a note? I don't see a note. There has to be a note."

Betty skimmed the front and back of the dress. "No note. Oh, wait, there's a second bag." She pulled it off the bar. "It's the mask, and I see a folded sheet of paper at the bottom."

She scooped out the black-velvet mask embellished with gold beading and a black feather and handed them to me. Reaching deeper into the bag, she fumbled for the note.

I held the mask in front of my face, flipping my hair off my shoulders, and asked, "How does it look?"

She assessed me before answering, "Captivating and quite mysterious."

Curtsying, I said, "Thank you, my lady." I lowered the mask, my curiosity getting the best of me. "What does the note say?"

Pulling out the folded sheet of gold paper, she broke the seal and read aloud: "Who better to portray the beautiful queen of France, Marie Antoinette, than you, my dear, Beth; therefore, it is only fitting Philippe come dressed as King Louis the XVI. All my love, Ptah. P.S. No mask = No right of entry." She closed the note and told me, "You'll make a lovely Marie Antoinette, Beth."

I'd heard of the queen but didn't know much about her history. Eyeing the elaborate gown, I gathered she was something of a fashion icon for that period. I snapped my head up. "Wait. What did he say about Philippe?"

Betty glanced at the paper and then at me. "He'll be going as King Louis XVI."

"Do you see a second costume?"

Betty shrugged her shoulders. "All I see is your dress."

I handed my mask to Betty and pushed my dress aside. A flash of gold caught my eye. At the very back I discovered a brilliantly gold majestic coat, with a blue slash draped across the front. White ruffles peeked through the lapel and cuffs. "Found it," I said, pulling the costume off the bar and holding it up for her to see.

Betty chuckled. "Are those white leggings or long johns under it?"

I burst out laughing. "They look like ballet tights, and what's up with this wig? Did men really wear rolled curls on the sides of their head?"

She gave it the once over, smothered a laugh under her hand, and then said, "I'm sure Philippe will look dashing, no matter how ridiculous it looks on the hanger." From the bag she produced a gold mask with blue etching. "At least the mask is rather attractive."

"He'll make it look fabulous, Betty."

"I'm sure you both will be a stunning pair," she said, and then ushered me toward the stairs. "Now get out of my hair. I've got work to do, and you need to get some rest before the party."

"Okay, okay, I'm going." I bounced up the stairs, stopped halfway, and turned to look down at her. "Thank you, Betty."

She shook her head. "For what?"

"Taking care of me."

"No need to thank me, dear. You're family." She waved both hands at me. "Now, shoo."

She was right. We were family, along with Philippe, Ptah, and even Caleb. They were at my side, seeing me through the loneliness, and tonight, for just a little while, I would leave my troubled life behind and become a magnificent queen.

****

Dressed in full gala attire, I stood with my gaze fixated on the stranger staring back from the floor-length mirror. Somewhere beneath the enormous wig, theatrical mask, and flaring gown was the person I'd always known...me, Beth, formerly human and presently vampire, neither of which was evident in this getup.

Betty seemed concerned. "What's the matter? You've been staring at yourself for quite some time."

I sighed loudly, allowing my shoulders to slump. "It's not me. I don't feel at all like me."

She raised her brows. "It's a masquerade ball, dear. You're not supposed to look at all like yourself."

Fumbling with the layers of ruffles, I explained, "I get that, but this is too much. The wig weighs a ton, and the dress is impossible to walk in. Obviously, the designers of this era weren't thinking about ease or fun when they created this bulky style."

Betty gave me a gentle nudge toward the bedroom door. "You couldn't wait for this night to arrive. Now it's here, and you've just got the jitters for some reason." She stepped out into the hallway and waved me forward. "You're going to have a wonderful time. You'll see."

I crossed the threshold. "I don't know."

She patted my hands. "You will. Come now, Philippe and Caleb are waiting in the foyer." She winked at me. "Once you get a load of them, you won't feel so awkward."

I clutched her arm. "Tell me. Is it that bad?"

She held up some fingers in front of her face. "On a scale from one to ten, it's an eight." She chuckled and shook her head. "I just can't get over those silly tights. But don't let them know. They're strutting around like peacocks."

I burst out laughing, quickly stifled my delight, and mimicked the grandeur of a queen. Holding my head high, I glided down the hallway toward the staircase. Glancing back at Betty and making a zipping motion over my lips, I said, "They won't hear it from me."

Turning back and descending the staircase, my gaze fell upon the two kings parading about the foyer. Philippe was clad in brilliant gold and Caleb in flamboyant red. When I reached the bottom, both came to an abrupt stop, crashing into one another.

I spun in a circle. "Do you like?"

Philippe rushed forward and kissed my cheek. "Beth, Ptah chose well. You're a stunning Marie Antoinette."

I curtsied. "Why, thank you, Louis."

Philippe bowed and then stood tall, gesturing toward Caleb. "May I present the King of Spain, Philip II."

Caleb lifted an enormous pirate's hat off his sheep-like wig and bowed. His lips spread into a devious grin. "My lady."

I gave him my most noble nod of acknowledgement.

Philippe elbowed Caleb out of his way and took my hand. "Jon Paul has the car running," he said, escorting me to the front door, opening it wide enough for my dress to fit through.

Caleb strolled onto the porch with his arms folded behind his back, and then glanced at the BMW. "That dress, along with the three of us, simply cannot fit inside the car."

"I guess you'll be walking then," I fired back.

"Not likely," he answered sarcastically.

"Don't start, you two," Philippe said, jerking down one of his cuffs. "Caleb, sit in the front with Jon Paul."

Jon Paul's eyes popped as they skimmed over my costume. He jogged over to the rear of the car, reaching down to gather up my skirt. He gave me a bemused smile. "Marie Antoinette, right?"

"Yes," I answered.

"Very convincing."

With his assistance, I managed to squeeze all of me and the layers of dress into the back of the car. "Thank you, Jon Paul," I said, struggling with the awkwardness of the costume.

Jon Paul stepped aside, allowing Philippe to climb in after me. Caleb turned in his seat and opened his mouth, but Philippe cut him off.

"Think before you speak, Caleb," Philippe warned. "One smartass comment and you *are* walking."

Caleb sprouted a wide grin. "I was only going to remark on what a lovely couple you make."

"Yeah, right," I said in a huff.

Philippe turned his attention to Jon Paul. "The gala's at Ptah's. Please take us there."

"Yes, Mr. Delon," he said, starting the engine.

As Jon Paul pulled out of our driveway, Philippe asked, "So, what's the game plan? Are we staying awhile or just making a brief appearance?"

Before I spoke a single word, Caleb rattled off, "I didn't throw on this cumbersome getup just to make an appearance. Besides, Ptah will expect us to stay."

"My costume is bulkier and more uncomfortable than either of yours," I pointed out. "The sooner I get out of this thing, the better."

Philippe weighed each hand in the air. "One wants to stay; one wants to go. What to do?"

I threw him a hard glare. "What do *you* choose?" *It'd better be in my favor.*

Philippe avoided eye contact with both me and Caleb. "Let's see how the night plays out and go from there. Fair enough?"

"Fair enough," Caleb echoed.

"Meh, whatever you think," I said, turning away and repressing a groan. I should have listened to my better judgment, abandoned the gown, and curled up with a good book; yet here I was clothed in absurdly clumsy garments swiftly approaching Ptah's doorstep. To hell with it. Philippe and Caleb could stay all night if it suited them. I'd make an appearance, roam the length of the house a time or two, and then quietly slip out the back to retreat to the solitude of our home.

Jon Paul swung the car to the right, following the private road leading up to the circular driveway surrounding Ptah's mansion. The pop of the passenger door being opened went off like a grenade inside my head. Jon Paul pushed it wide open and took both my hands. "I'm going to lift you out."

Philippe wadded up the bulk of my dress from behind and said, "I'll push, you pull, Jon Paul."

The skirt sprang open like a trap once I'd climbed free. A gentle sea breeze, spiked with the rich scent of blood, encircled me, tickling my throat and tempting my fangs. I swayed.

Jon Paul clung to my hands as if I'd blow away with the wind.

"I'm fine, Jon Paul," I said. "You can let go now."

Philippe placed his hand in the small of my back. "Thank you, Jon Paul."

Jon Paul's smile was kind. He released me and took a step backward. "You're quite welcome, sir."

Caleb hopped out of the car, smoothing down his jacket and rubbing his hands together. "Showtime, folks."

"I'm sure you'll provide us with some kind of performance, won't you, Caleb?" I teased.

His customary devilish grin surfaced. "You know me too well, Beth."

I merely rolled my eyes.

Philippe stepped between us. "Enough." Turning to Jon Paul, he said, "I'll reach out to you when we're ready to leave."

"Very well, sir," he replied.

I kept the car in my sight as it vanished over the hill. Even then, I didn't budge.

Philippe laced our fingers, steering me toward the house. "Let's get inside. I'm dying for a glass of warm blood."

I licked my lips. "That does sound lovely."

Caleb took a wide stance, planting his feet firmly on the ground. Stretching his arms out wide, he shouted into the night, "The house is brimming with the scent of blood." He sprinted forward, vanishing into the darkness.

The invitation had made no mention of blood being served. Sticking my nose in the air and sniffing like a dog, I pursued the thick, salty bouquet all the way up to the porch and through the open front door.

Once inside the game room transformed into the ballroom, I observed hordes of masked kings and queens parading across the polished floor. From the adjacent ballroom, the soft sigh of violins composed a tragic piece. I couldn't be bothered with any of that; I craved the scent of blood seasoning the air. Where was the damn smell coming from? My gaze wandered in frustration.

A flash of deep scarlet caught my eye, and I jerked my head in its direction. An ivory fountain, in my sights for a split second, peeked between the meandering nobles. Pushing through the crowd, I made my pursuit. The fountain sat dead center of the room. Streams of creamy blood spilled over its rim, splashing into the egg-shaped basin.

I shuddered with delight and brushed the chill from my arms. As I gazed at its glory, the surrounding guests faded into the background. Only the cascade of blood remained. I managed to reach the fountain in a single forward bound. To its right, engraved goblets lined a glass table. Among them I discovered one with my name etched across the center. As my fingertips curled around the stem, saliva flooded my mouth. I hurriedly shoved the goblet under a steady stream of blood, filling it to the rim. I tipped my head back so the warm, sweet blood could flow over my tongue. I didn't stop, not even to take a breath. I just drank, consuming every last drop.

Images blurred around me, but with every blink my vision grew sharper, clearer. The boisterous swarm of kings and queens reemerged. I hadn't budged an inch, claiming my spot by the fang-rousing fountain. Caleb stood at my left and Philippe on my right, both gulping down their own goblets of blood. Philippe's medieval suits of armor, stationed at the fountain, guarded each side.

Philippe turned his eyes on me, a radiant glow spreading across his cheeks. "That was almost sinful," he said, wiping his lips.

I gave him a playful nudge.

Caleb clapped his hands then rubbed them together. "Now that my thirst is satisfied , I'm ready to crush everyone in a fencing duel." He indicated Philippe. "Even you."

Philippe gave a firm shake of his head. "Not a chance."

Caleb smirked. "Intimidated by my mad skills?"

"I should stay with Beth. You go ahead."

Caleb's eyes widened. "You're kidding, right?"

Touching Philippe's arm, I said, "Go with Caleb. I'll be fine."

Enclosing my hands in his, he bent to gaze into my eyes. "You're sure?"

"Of course," I answered, waving him away.

He couldn't contain his impish grin any longer. "Thank you," he said, before kissing my cheek.

Caleb grabbed Philippe's shoulder. "Let's go."

Philippe trotted backward, blowing me a kiss before he and Caleb vanished into the crowd. My gaze lingered on the hallway as if Philippe might decide to come rushing back to me. After a few moments, I set out to explore the remaining rooms.

A sea of kings and queens, clothed in an assortment of vibrant colors, strutted throughout the room. Zigzagging between them, I inched my way toward the table along the left wall, stacked with appetizers. The whole scene was breathtaking. High-backed marble thrones lined the walls, offering stately resting points for scores of party-weary guests. A small orchestra—comprised of about thirty pieces—monopolized the far-right corner, filling the room with the enchantment of string, brass, and woodwind instruments. Overhead, glass-blown crystal chandeliers bedecked the cathedral ceiling, illuminating the brilliant costumes swirling around the dance floor.

"Marie Antoinette, right?" a male voiced asked at my right ear.

Turning, I found myself staring into the masked face of a king clad in a high-collared scarlet jacket embroidered in gold. His hand rested atop the handle of an intricately-cast sword, which hung loose at his side. Lifting his chin and holding his head high, he announced, "I'm Napoleon Bonaparte. Yes, I am an emperor, not a king, but isn't emperor the superior title?"

I was far from impressed. "Is it? I wouldn't know."

He chuckled. "Yes, as a matter of fact, it is." Reaching out his hand, he introduced himself non-fictionally. "I'm Mark, and you are?"

Taking his hand, I responded, "Beth."

He bowed and said, "It would be my honor, Beth, if I may have one dance."

I glanced toward the dance floor then back at the stranger. His light-blue eyes gleaming behind the black mask were definitely human. The river of delicious blood coursing through his veins throbbed inside my head, but I *had* already fed. Surely one dance couldn't hurt.

"Dance with me." he pleaded again, clasping my hands.

Shaking my head, I said, "I'd better not. I came with my husband."

He looked around, exaggerated confusion written into his expression "Oh? Where is he?"

"Fencing," I said with a bored sigh.

"Fool." Eyeing the neckline of my dress, he said, "You're very beautiful. I can't let you leave without sharing a dance—just one."

I slammed my hands onto my hips. "It's my dress that caught your eye, not my beauty."

"You're wrong. Yes, your dress is quite seductive and distracting, but it's your eyes I find myself most captivated by. They sparkle as if they were jewels. I can't take my eyes off them. You're a vampire, yes?"

I narrowed my gaze and replied, "I am."

Grabbing my hand, he pulled me forward and wrapped his other arm around my waist. "Will you bite me?" he whispered into my ear.

His racing heartbeat tempted my fangs, but I pushed him away. I wasn't here to feed. "If you want to be bitten, go to Bloodthirst."

He boldly stepped closer to me, licked his lips, and then whispered, "It's *your* bite I want."

I grabbed him by the throat. With vampire speed I shoved him backward, pinning him against the wall. His eyes bulged as he clawed at my hand. I let him squirm. The blood slowly drained from his face and his expression twisted in horror. I brushed my lips across his cheek and whispered, "Be careful what you wish for. It might just come true." I loosened my grip then and finally released him.

Gasping, he clutched his neck. "You could have killed me!"

I shrugged my shoulders and pointed out, "I merely taught you a lesson."

He stumbled backward. Jutting out a rigid finger, he shouted, "You're crazy," before bolting from the room.

Yawning, I watched him go and then continued, exiting the ballroom. In a slow, steady gait, I crossed the foyer and headed toward the staircase. A spirited group of kings and queens congregated at the foot of the stairs. They bellowed with laughter as they guzzled wine, splattering it down the front of their clothes. Fixing my eyes on their camouflaged faces, I heaved a heavy sigh. Other than the masked faces and colorful garments, not a single soul stood apart amidst the masquerade of royalty. The partygoers were nothing more than strangers, and without the slightest bit of concern for me or my predicament. Like everything else, the gala only served to magnify my pain, suffering, and loneliness. I stuck out like a sore thumb, alone, damaged, and in need of the comforts of alcohol. I ducked beneath the staircase and slumped against the wall, lowering my head.

"Hello, Beth."

The divine voice, smooth and rich like fine wine, crept into my ears. I stood completely still, my gaze locked on the floor, my brain scrambling to hold a sane thought. *No, it couldn't be, could it? Am I hearing things? Have I gone mad? Dear God, please don't play cruel tricks on me.* I raised my head in a painfully slow manner. A pair of black shoes came into view, then white tights, then a pleated gold skirt. My gaze darted upward, traveling like wildfire over his high-collared burgundy jacket, to the tips of his dark-ringlet wig, to finally rest upon a gold-leaf mask framing two striking emerald-green eyes.

My mouth gaped open. I struggled to speak but couldn't call forth a single word. Trembling, I rooted my feet into the floor and pressed my hands against the wall, searching for the strength to remain standing.

"Are you not happy to see me?" Amon asked, taking a step closer.

The word yes spun around my head several times before finally making it out of my mouth. "Yes." I squeezed my eyelids shut to blink away my tears before drinking him with my eyes. "God, yes!"

With the grace and speed of a god he approached, stopping millimeters from me. He tore away his mask, tossing it aside, and then slipped his fingers behind my ears to unfasten mine. My mask fell to the floor, but our eyes never left each other to trace its descent. With the back of his hand, he stroked my cheek. "I have missed gazing into your eyes, my darling Beth."

My heartbeat quickened, pumping blood faster and faster into my veins. A rush of adrenaline spurred me forward. Standing on my tiptoes and cupping his face in my hands, I covered his mouth with mine and kissed him as though I might never take another breath.

His arms encircled my waist, pulling me into his embrace while his body crushed me against the wall. Our tongues softly caressed, intertwining as though they were of one flesh. He kissed me harder, stronger, and with such urgency it set my soul aflame. I clung to him, terrified to let go. The years of torment and unease of not knowing where he was resurfaced from where I'd tried to lock them away. A waterfall of hot tears cascaded down my cheeks. I couldn't turn them off. I couldn't fight the sorrow. It defeated me, and I surrendered.

Plucking my wig from my head, he unpinned my hair, smoothing it with his hands and whispering, "It's okay, Beth. I'm here."

His breath on my ear, his heartbeat pounding on top of mine, and the strength of his arms around me breathed life back into my broken soul; yet, a cold, hard truth gripped at my stomach. All that time, he was with Hathor. I pushed him away. "You left me for her!"

He gently kissed my cheek and reassured me. "I did no such thing. Isis's magic controlled me. I have no recollection of those years. One day I suddenly came to, like waking from a coma. Isis, Hathor, and Osiris took one look at me and scattered like rats. My only thought was to run back to you...and here I am."

The conviction in his voice rang in my ears, mending every frazzled nerve. He held me for some time, stroking my back and hair. I gathered my composure and wiped my face, finally pulling away from him. I pinched my arm. *I'm not dreaming. He's here, standing in front of me.* Like every other king, he looked ridiculous in those silly tights. A light bulb went off. How could he be in gala attire? I narrowed my eyes and anchored a hand on my hip. "When did you get back? How did you know to find me here? Better yet, why are you in costume? Who told you about the gala? Was it Ptah? Did you go to him before you came to *me*?"

He pressed a finger to my lips. "May I answer?"

I gave a curt nod.

He stood with his arms limp at his sides. "It's been five years. I had no idea how you would react to me."

Throwing my hands up in frustration, I blurted out, "How can you say that? I waited years for your return. I drank continuously to numb my pain." My eyes swelled with tears. I swallowed hard. "Every second of every day I was in agony, not knowing where you were."

He placed his hands on my shoulders and focused his gaze on my eyes. "Beth, I was *with* Hathor. Even under the influence of magic, I was ashamed of my betrayal. I couldn't be sure you would welcome me with open arms. I went to Ptah to learn of your feelings. It was he who suggested I surprise you at the gala."

I shook my head and broke eye contact. "Ptah took care of me and kept my faith alive. He knew one day you would return to me."

He lifted my chin, locking his eyes on mine once more. "I must thank him, as he knows nothing could keep me away from you, not even a silly spell."

My thoughts scattered. Too excited to think straight, I couldn't form words to speak, only react. Wrapping my arms around his neck, I hugged him with all my might. Suddenly, I found my voice. "None of that matters, only here and now."

He stripped off his wig, his jet-black hair tumbling down and spilling over his shoulders. Embracing me once more, he breathed, "I love you."

"And I you," I whispered back.

His lips nuzzled my neck, inching up my throat to caress my mouth. Drunk on his kiss, I swayed in his arms.

"I could stay like this forever," he admitted; yet, in the next moment, he released me. Holding me at arm's length, I could see his eyes go stone cold. "I was not set free, Beth, but quite the opposite. As I said, one day the magic simply vanished, as did Osiris, Hathor, and Isis. I mean to find them. They must pay for their crimes."

I took his hand, interlocking our fingers. "And I will stand by your side. We all will. Ptah, Caleb, Philippe, and I took a vow the night you disappeared. We promised to help you seek vengeance against them."

"I'd snap their necks if given the chance. But I do not govern them. The Council must decide their fate. My role is to deliver them, but first I must find them."

I let out an impatient huff. "Ptah has searched far and wide. He couldn't find you or them. It will even be harder now."

In a steady voice, he affirmed, "We *will* find them. Are you certain you're with me?"

"Of course, I am."

That made him smile. "Wonderful. Let's go find the others. We must compose a strategy."

CHAPTER 5

Word of Amon's return spread like wildfire. The gala ran late, but finally only the five of us remained: Ptah, Caleb, Philippe, Amon, and I. With our masks and wigs set aside, we gathered together in the living room. Ptah claimed a spot by the window, standing as straight and rigid as an arrow. Caleb faded into the background, his arms crossed over his chest and his gaze ping ponging between Philippe and Amon. Philippe hovered close to me, smoothing and re-smoothing his hand over his jacket. Amon settled into an over-sized chair adjacent to the sofa, hooking his arm over the back of the seat. I perched on the edge of the snake-shaped leather sofa, rapidly clasping and unclasping my hands.

No one spoke, and the swelling silence crept into every corner of the room. Every sound agitated my vampire hearing; the exchange of breath, the beat of multiple hearts, creaks uttered by the house, the whisper of the wind through the trees outside, the crash of waves against the shore. I pressed my fingertips against my temples, closing my eyes and making an attempt to massage away the clamor of useless noise. *Damn it, somebody say something!*

Amon's heavenly voice entered my head, *I will, my love.*

My gaze darted toward him, and I dropped my restless hands into my lap.

Amon leaned back in the chair and placed his hands behind his head. "I'm back."

Philippe made a dramatic gesture with his arm. "That's it? No apology, no admittance of guilt, just, *'I'm back'?*"

Amon rose slowly to his feet, hooking his thumbs in the waistband of his tights. "I was spelled, with no control over my own actions. Why should I apologize?"

Philippe's nostrils flared. "You don't know what I've…" His head jerked in my direction. "What Beth's been through these past five years. An apology is the least you could do."

A sense of calm flowed through my body. In my eyes, Amon didn't have to utter a single syllable. The kiss we'd shared had said it all. I needed no apology.

Amon's expression softened. He lowered his head, and then raised it high. "Of course, I feel regret for anyone who has suffered on my behalf. I have every intention of making it up to those wronged, but Beth does not hold me responsible." He spread his arms wide as his gaze traveled the room. "Isn't that why we are all here, to avenge the injustice we suffered at the hands of Osiris, Isis, and Hathor?"

Ptah left his post by the window to stand by Amon's side. "Yes, of course."

Philippe tightened his jaw, then relaxed his expression. "Make no mistake, I'm here for Beth. I do this only for her."

Amon gave a slight nod. "Understood."

Caleb approached Philippe and then faced Amon, thrusting out his chest. "We took a vow, and we will honor that oath," he declared. "Now, where do we begin?"

Ptah shook a finger in the air. "That is precisely the question." He looked directly at Amon. "I interrogated everyone we know, inspected every corner of any possible hiding place to learn of your whereabouts, and still came up empty handed. Even The Council, whose reach extends to places unknown, were at a loss. With their sins out in the open they will dig deeper underground, and most likely, a blanket of Isis's magic shields them."

"What about a locator spell?" I asked.

Ptah cracked a half smile, and then snapped his fingers. "What we need is a damned witch. Unfortunately, the best of the lot burned at the stake in sixteen ninety-two."

The subject of witches brought Margarete to mind, and I offered a suggestion. "We should ask Margarete."

"You think she knows a witch?" Amon asked, kneeling before me and brushing a strand of hair from my face to tuck behind my ear.

Peering into his perfect emerald-green eyes, I ached to touch him.

Philippe pulled me to my feet and away from Amon, adding, "Maybe we should leave Margarete out of this. She's a bit off."

Amon rose as well and then questioned, "You mean she's unstable?"

"She did refuse the gala invitation," Ptah pointed out. "Stated she wasn't a fan of masks. I thought it rather odd."

"Nonsense," Caleb said with a knowing grin. "Margarete is rather extraordinary and dabbles in the spirit world. She's probably our best bet at finding a witch."

Ptah scratched his beard. "Then she might be an invaluable ally."

Amon looked at me. "Do you agree, Beth?"

"I do."

Amon winked. "Then we shall go see her."

"And we shall," Ptah agreed, "but not tonight. It's late. We're all exhausted. Stay; I have plenty of room. Tomorrow, we speak with Margarete."

Amon clapped Ptah on the back. "Tomorrow it is." He turned to me and held out his hand. "Let us retire."

My lovesick heart pounded out a rhythm of eager anticipation. Spreading my hand over my chest, I struggled to smother the over-excited thumping, but my heart wanted what it had missed out on for over 1,825 days. Just as I was about to rise and place my hand in Amon's, Philippe pushed me aside and stood between us.

"She's not going upstairs with you."

Amon exuded arrogance. "She is."

Philippe jabbed his finger into Amon's chest. "She's *my* wife. She'll go with me."

Amon crossed his arms confidently, throwing Philippe's finger aside. "And she's *my* immortal companion."

I sank further into the couch, my eyes bouncing back and forth between Amon and Philippe.

Ptah pinched the bridge of his nose and heaved a great sigh. "Wrangling for Beth's hand isn't the answer. This can't be a struggle for power."

"I'm inclined to agree," Caleb chimed in.

Amon radiated superiority their way. "As I recall, Philippe and I agreed to share Beth's affections." Amon glared at Philippe. "You've had her for five years. It's my turn now."

Philippe barked, "You show up out of the blue and expect to take over. No way. Ain't gonna happen."

I leapt to my feet, exasperated. "Enough. I'm not some kind of trophy you can pass back and forth." I smoothed out my skirt and raised my chin in defiance. "I'm going upstairs—*alone*."

Amon lifted a single brow. "You can't be serious. You want to be with me. I felt it in your kiss."

Philippe blinked rapidly and then faced me. "You kissed him?"

Amon bragged, "Twice."

A visible flush rose in Philippe's cheeks. He puffed out his chest with pride. "She's kissed me thousands of times."

Caleb shoved his hands into his pockets and shrugged his shoulders. "She kissed me once."

All heads, including mine, whipped in Caleb's direction. I emitted a frustrated snort. "That was years ago, and *you* kissed *me!*"

Ptah scratched his forehead and mused, "She's never kissed me."

I threw my hands up and groaned. "For the love of God, you're immature little boys. And at the moment, none of you are worth my time." With a sharp turn I sought the solitude of one of the many bedrooms upstairs. Taking the stairs two at a time, I reached the second level, blew them all a haughty kiss, and then ducked down the hallway.

I was no stranger to Ptah's home. I knew every inch as if it were my own. Curling up in my usual spot on the sofa was out of the question, especially with the four of them hovering over me. I'd have to make do with one of the bedrooms—all of which were decorated extravagantly, like rooms at a five-star resort, complete with giant canopy beds covered in pillows, luxurious soaker tubs, heated floors, and fluffy terrycloth robes.

I stopped in front of the fourth door along the hallway, pushed it open, and stepped inside. The scent of lavender and peaches perfumed the air, awakening my senses. Stripping off the bulky gown and padding across the deliciously warm floors, I headed into the bathroom, where I cranked the hot water and filled the tub. I sank down into its escape, resting my head against the fully inflated bath pillow at the back. I purred like a cat who had no desire to be anywhere else.

I lingered until the water cooled, matching the temperature of my skin. The downy robe hanging on the back of the door waited for me to slip inside. I tightened its sash before strolling into the bedroom.

"Darling," Amon addressed me with a light-hearted, teasing tone.

He sat cross-legged in the chair facing the bed, resting his elbows on the arms and his fingertips forming a steeple. As he gazed at me, a playful grin crossed his lips, and he licked them like a wolf preparing to gobble me up. "You look utterly ravishing."

Pressing my fingers over my lips, I attempted to hide my delight. "What are you doing here? Did I not say I wanted to be alone?"

He leaned back in the chair and placed his hand on his chest. "Surely that did not apply to me." He winked. "That smile you're hiding tells me so."

I burst out laughing, dropping my hand away as I fought to compose myself. "It doesn't matter what you or I want. We have to consider Philippe's feelings."

"Why? We are bound by blood. His emotions mean nothing."

"I will not hurt him," I vowed.

He stood, puffing his chest out, and strutted across the floor like a magnificent lion. Stopping in front of me, he locked his eyes on mine. "Will you hurt me?"

My temperature rose. I ached all over, craving his touch, inching closer. "No, of course not."

His lips softly brushed mine as he murmured, "Then we are at an impasse."

My breath quickened. "I don't have the solution."

Our lips slammed together in a sudden fervent and impatient rush. His wet tongue slipped into my mouth, and I welcomed it greedily. Scooping me up in his arms, he carried me to the bed and lay with me, his body atop mine. The temptation to touch him, explore him, lose myself in him consumed me down to my bones; yet, I was unable to surrender my heart. With every ounce of strength I could call forth, I turned my head and pushed Amon away. In a flat tone, I said, "We can't. I can't."

Amon's passionate breaths slowed. He gazed at me for some time before nodding his assent. "I understand, but at least let me stay here with you and hold you in my arms as we sleep."

Staring down at my hands, I shook my head. "If you stay, we both know what will happen." I gave him a nudge. "You have to go. I'm sorry."

He sat very still, hanging his head. A crushing weight splintered my heart in two. I longed to comfort him, reach for him, and it required all my willpower, not to mention sitting on my hands, not to do so.

He sighed in defeat and climbed from the bed. Facing the doorway, he murmured, "Good night, Beth."

"Good night," I said, pulling my knees into my chest and hugging them so my arms wouldn't remain empty.

****

When I awoke the next morning, Philippe occupied the very chair Amon had the night before. He'd shed his costume from the night before in favor of khakis and a plaid shirt. Dark circles plagued his handsome face. A duffle bag rested by his feet, and he cradled a steaming mug in both hands as if trying to warm them. He smiled. "Hi."

Sitting up, I leaned back into the mountain of pillows piled along the headboard. "Hi." Frowning, I asked, "Didn't you sleep?"

He gave a quick shake of his head before rising to his feet. "Couldn't." He came and sat on the bed, handing me the mug of blood. "I was ashamed of how I behaved last night." His gaze lingered on my face as if he were taking a mental picture. "I'm sorry."

As I took the mug my finger brushed lightly against his. "Everyone was behaving out of sorts. Smells delicious." I used the mug to defer the subject of conversation and took a healthy sip, closing my eyes as the blood slid down my throat.

"I brought you a change of clothes," he said, snapping my attention back to him.

I glanced at the duffle bag. "You've been home already? What time is it? Did I oversleep?"

"Right after sundown, I went home to shower, change, and pick up some clothes for you. You were still asleep when I came back at around six-thirty, so I headed downstairs to drink a mug of blood with the guys before bringing this one back up for you. It's only now a little after seven."

I ran my hand through my hair, smoothing it down. "Everyone's still downstairs?"

He gave a halfhearted shrug. "Think so. Ptah's hell-bent on going to Bloodthirst. Wants to see if Margarete can put us in touch with a witch."

I eyed him over the rim of the mug. "You don't agree?"

"Well, you know her better than me, but it does seem a bit farfetched."

"Perhaps, but we don't have a lot of options, do we? I say we go and find out for certain."

Pursing his lips, he pulled at his goatee. "Fair enough." He moved to scoop up the duffle bag and then set it on the edge of the bed. "Here are your clothes. I'll let the others know you'll be down shortly."

Tossing the covers aside, I jumped out of bed and swung the duffle bag over my shoulder. "Gonna take a quick shower. I'll meet you downstairs."

"Okay," he said, slipping out of the bedroom and closing the door behind him.

In less than ten minutes I'd showered, dressing in the jeans, gray V-neck T-shirt, and black boots Philippe had brought. I tied my hair back in a ponytail, then went in pursuit of the others.

Halfway down the stairs Amon's angelic voice reached me. My pulse skyrocketed and the urge to race down the stairs so I could plant my lips on top of his overtook me. Grabbing onto the banister, I attempted to calm my unrelenting heart. It only drummed more violently inside my chest, professing its love for the entire world to hear. I couldn't let my impulsive declaration of love reach Philippe's ears, nor did I want him to see me like this. I closed my eyes, inhaling and exhaling slowly, while picturing serene landscapes, imagining I was standing inside them without a care in the world.

"Beth," Philippe called out.

My eyes snapped open to find Philippe with a foot on the first stair. A bewildered look greeted me. "Are you all right?"

I laughed nervously then cleared my throat. "I'm fine." I tucked away my thoughts of Amon for safe keeping and trotted down the stairs to land before him.

He studied me, his posture relaxing and a slow smile growing on his lips. "Come," he said, holding out his hand. "Everyone is in the living room."

I took his hand and smiled back. Apparently, he was none the wiser of my spontaneous surge of affections toward Amon. Whatever would I do without my black chest of secrets?

Side by side we walked through the foyer, approaching the living room. Just outside the entrance he dropped my hand in favor of my arm so he could pull me aside. He cleared his throat and said, "You're lovestruck right now. I get it."

I was wrong. My attempt to hide my feelings had failed miserably.

"Amon just got back." He took both my hands into his. "I'm still here. I know it hasn't been easy for us, and I've been a jerk, but we were trying. Do keep in mind that, truly, you know nothing about him."

I retreated from him. "Don't tell me what I know or don't know. Furthermore, I've known him all my life."

"Okay, so what are his habits, his ambitions, his dreams, his failures? Do you even know?" He made a good point.

"Well, I...I...I'll learn them."

"Don't rush forward blindly. All I ask is that you give it time; give me time."

"Rushing? I've waited all my life. I hardly call that rushing."

"That's what you do," he accused. "You act. You don't think. For God's sake, you moved in with me days after we met."

"Because I thought you were him," I fired back.

"Exactly my point. Taking a walk along the cliffs that very first night, I just happened upon you and Danny. Your mind was an open book. I read it in seconds."

I glared at him. "You used me."

He raised his brows and placed a hand on his chest. "Me? It was you. You used me. Anyone could have shown up claiming to be Amon. It wouldn't have mattered. You believed I was him because it suited your needs, your desires. You wanted it, him, to be real."

I rubbed at my forehead in agitation. "Stop; just stop." My eyes bore into his. "Yes, maybe I was foolish and naïve, and of course I wanted to believe, but *you* took advantage of my vulnerability. You played me."

He kneaded the back of his neck as if it pained him. "And I've apologized over and over and over again. If you knew Amon, really knew him, I couldn't have deceived you. So, I'll say it again; you don't know him."

Crossing my arms, I spat, "No, I don't know *you*."

He lowered his voice. "You do. You fell in love with me; not him, me."

I stood a little taller. Bringing my face close to his, I said, "I did. I fell in love with you, but hear me now, Philippe; I *know* Amon. I love him. It was just easier for me to rationalize all the inconsistencies because I wanted so badly to believe."

"So you admit you fell for me?"

Somehow he'd blocked out everything else I'd said, so why bother to repeat it? He'd heard the words he'd wanted to and fixated on them. I heaved a sigh. "Yes."

Again, he took my hands and brought them to his lips, kissing them sweetly. "What we have is real. Our love is real. Remember that. Give us some serious thought before you make a final decision."

He stared at me with raw unspoken pain, and its force pierced my soul. For five years he'd stood by me, vowed to avenge the wrong done to all of us—including Amon—and that night so very long ago, we'd sworn to stay together no matter what. "I will."

He slumped forward, releasing a breath in relief. Hugging me close, he murmured, "Thank you."

Gently, I pulled away, staring at him intently. "My love for Amon is also real. You must remember that."

His posture stiffened as he answered, "Of that I'm well aware."

Caleb emerged from the living room and approached us. He tilted his chin downward and frowned. "Are you two at it again? Enough. Come with me; we're all waiting."

As I passed by him, I bit my tongue to stifle a snide remark.

"Stay out of it," Philippe warned.

Caleb smirked, holding up his hands in defeat. "Fine."

Ptah sat on the edge of the sofa clad in faded jeans and a white linen shirt. Amon, seated to his right, looked rather GQ in his white jeans, gray-and-white-striped shirt, and a gray jean jacket. His eyes were so bright they could've become the sun in the sky.

A weightless feeling ran through me and I longed for the taste of his mouth, but I'd just promised Philippe I'd give him and me serious thought.

"Now that we're all here, what's the plan?" Philippe asked, coming to my side and placing his hand in the small of my back.

I swallowed hard and forced a smile. No matter what I conjured up inside my head to dissuade myself, every inch of my body craved Amon's touch.

Ptah pushed off the sofa and shook a finger in the air. "We go to Bloodthirst, but first we drink." With vampire swiftness he bolted from the room, then returned carrying a tray filled with five goblets. Setting it down on the coffee table, he commanded, "Drink."

Caleb rubbed his hands together, wasting no time in scooping up a glass. "Blood. Wonderful."

I bent down and selected mine. I closed my eyes and savored the taste.

Ptah chugged the contents of his in one gulp.

Philippe grabbed his own goblet. He raised it in Ptah's direction. "Thank you."

Amon claimed the last remaining glass. He came to me, tapped our goblets, and whispered in my ear, "To us."

The hairs rose on the back of my neck, and I shifted closer to him. "To us," I echoed only for his ears.

"Finish up, people. Let's not waste time," Ptah shouted, snapping his fingers to rouse us.

"Are we flying or driving?" Caleb asked.

"Flying," Ptah and Amon chimed together.

"Driving," Philippe said seconds after.

Amon winked at me, grabbed my hand, and said, "Hold on tight."

We shot out the front door before anyone could utter a single word. My head spun with the speed, but the thrill of it made me squeal with glee. He pulled me close as we drifted past the clouds. Our lips met, soft, wet, and full of hunger. I tasted every supple inch of his mouth on mine. A heated surge ignited between us. Warmth flooded my veins, stirring my nerves. Soft moans sounded in my ears...*my* moans. Miles above the ground, I found myself on the verge of surrendering to him completely. Suddenly, our pace slowed, and I found my feet on the ground. Feeling the sidewalk beneath my feet smothered the fever inside me.

Amon cupped my face in his hands. "God, I love you."

I breathed, "I love you too."

"Knock it off, lovebirds," Ptah called out.

My mouth went dry, and I held my breath. Was Philippe with him? Had he seen us kiss? I jerked my head around in the direction of Ptah's voice.

He was alone.

I exhaled with great relief. "Where's Philippe?" As an afterthought, I added, "And Caleb?"

Ptah rose up on his toes and shrugged his shoulders. "Philippe's not happy. That stunt you pulled, whisking Beth off like that, infuriated him. He's talking crazy; wants to fight you for Beth's hand. Caleb stayed behind to cool him off." Ptah frowned, pointing at me. "You can't keep this up. You need to make your choice."

Amon stuck out his chest and boomed with laughter. "Make her choice. Hah, done."

Ptah looked to me and said, "Let him down easy."

"Amon," I said in a soft voice, "I told Philippe I would give it some thought before I made my final decision."

Amon stood stock-still...not even his brow twitched. Then slowly, mechanically, he turned his head to face me. "You did what?"

"What was I supposed to do? I can't just say, 'Oh, Amon's back, so goodbye.' I'm his wife. I took vows."

Tension spread through his neck and shoulders, and he raised the volume of his voice. "And you're my immortal companion. Our blood binds us. The human ritual of marriage cannot compare."

I tenderly stroked his cheek. "I love you. It's always been you. Philippe needs time to come to terms with that. I owe him that much." I held back the fact that I had to come to terms with it as well.

He held my hand to his face and closed his eyes. Little by little, his posture relaxed. "Very well. But I will not wait long, Beth."

I matched his unyielding gaze and tone. "Nor will I."

A cocky smile played across his lips, and he kissed me ever so softly.

Ptah stepped between us, pushing us apart. "Focus, people. We're here to find a witch, not make out. And in public, no less." He swung his head in the direction of Bloodthirst's front doors. "Are we going in or do you wish to continue standing here all night?"

"Shouldn't we wait for Philippe and Caleb?" I asked.

Ptah looked exasperated. "It may be awhile before Philippe pulls himself together. I say we go in and have a quick chat with Margarete. Caleb and Philippe can meet us inside when they arrive."

"Sounds good to me," Amon said, taking my hand. "Beth, shall we go in?"

Truth be told, avoiding an awkward situation between Philippe and Amon got my vote. "Yes, let's go. They'll find us when they get here."

Ptah pulled the doors open. "After you," he said, ushering us inside.

The delicious aroma of human blood filled my nostrils as we crossed the threshold. I licked my lips and staggered like a drunk. Only a short time ago, I had consumed blood...had my fill even; yet the pulsating veins of the unsuspecting victims called to me, their life force beckoning me. My hunger intensified with each step, overriding all reason and morals.

Human nectar wafted through the air as vampires moaned. As Amon held tight to my hand, he guided me away from the entangled embrace of humans and vampires. "Do you see her, Beth?" he asked, breaking the trance.

Underneath the glow of a pendant lamp, her long raven hair caught my eye. She was seated in one of the circular black-velvet booths, edging closer to the man next to her. She revealed pearly fangs, which she slid along his neck. My ears rang with the thump of his heartbeat as she pierced his veins.

Respecting her privacy, I urged Amon and Ptah back a couple of steps. "She's feeding on someone."

"That can wait," Ptah said, zigzagging around me and jetting off in Margarete's direction.

I pursued, latching onto his arm and pulling him to a screeching halt mere inches from the booth. Amon followed quietly behind before taking his place at my side.

Oblivious to the audience around her, Margarete clung to the man, nursing the pulsating jugular on the side of his neck.

Ptah less than patiently cleared his throat.

Without so much as a glance in our direction, she swatted at the air as though we were pesky flies. Amon chuckled while Ptah drummed at the floor with his foot.

Margarete's gaze flicked upward and over the man's shoulder. The pallid hue of her perfect skin grew a shade paler, and her eyes grew with shock. She released the man, shoving him away. "Go," she barked. "Leave me."

The man tumbled out of the booth, glassy-eyed and dazed. A ridiculous grin crawled across his face as he gazed stupidly at her. "Thank you," he said, meandering off to vanish inside the crowd.

Margarete surprised me by lowering her head. Keeping her gaze fixed on the table, she spoke. "Supreme Ruler of the Undead, how may I be of service?"

Ptah groaned slightly. "My dear, I believe we've already settled this misconception of yours. A ruler I am not."

A gleam flashed in Amon's eyes. "I rather like the title."

Ptah turned his back on Amon to face Margarete. "We need your help. May we sit?"

"Yes, of course." She scooted to make room for all of us.

I slid in first, next to her. Amon followed, cradling me with his arm. Ptah climbed in opposite Margarete.

"My, my, my," she whispered in my ear. "When did Amon return? And where is Philippe?"

Leaning in, I mumbled, "I'll fill you in later."

Margarete sat upright, giving Ptah her full attention. "How may I help?"

He got right to the point. "We need a witch."

She didn't even flinch. "For what?"

Ptah paused to purse his lips before answering, "A locator spell."

"Who or what needs finding?"

Amon scowled when he said the names aloud. "Osiris, Isis, and Hathor."

A slow smirk formed on her lips. "Whose bright idea was it to engage a witch?"

Ptah stuck up his hand. "That would be me."

She frowned at the group. "No witch will go up against Isis. That would be suicide. She's far too powerful."

I asked, "Well then, what are we supposed to do? Got any suggestions?"

With her oddly beautiful purplish eyes fixated on the ceiling, she tapped her chin. Her finger froze, and she stiffened. "I know," she thought aloud.

"What do you know?" Ptah pressed.

Her eyes sharpened when the words crept from her mouth. "A demon has no fear."

My tone was incredulous. "A demon…really?"

She gave a curt nod. "I'm dead serious. A demon will not fear Isis. It is Isis who will fear the demon."

Hunting down a powerful demon was reckless. "We'd be fools to proceed with this course of action," I argued. "I mean, we'd be putting ourselves in danger. How could we control this demon?"

"Depends on the demon," Margarete said.

Amon regarded her with a sarcastic smile. "You do realize we want to survive this, right?"

Ptah held his hand up to silence Amon and leaned across the table. "I like it. Tell me more."

"Demons and dark spirits can be a very persuasive force against enemies; sometimes they do become quite violent." Margarete glanced at me. "And as Beth pointed out, they can't be controlled. You would be at their mercy."

Ptah's lips adopted a mischievous grin. "Where can I find one?"

Amon eyed Ptah in annoyance. "Did you not hear what she just said?"

"Unless you can come up with a better idea," Ptah challenged, "we're out of options."

Amon let out a snort of disgust. "I want retribution, but not at the risk of all our lives."

I squeezed Amon's forearm in a show of solidarity. "Whatever you decide, I'll stand by you."

"As will I," Ptah declared. "But there are five of us."

"It might come down to the three of us, since Caleb and Philippe still haven't shown up," Amon pointed out.

Ptah clapped Amon on the shoulder. "You and I are vampire gods, and Beth has your blood inside her. We can handle a single demon."

Amon looked at me, and I nodded my assent. "Where do we find such a demon?" he asked our host.

She gestured, indicating the crowd around them. "Bloodthirst seems to attract them. Maybe it's the smell of blood, or the number of free kills, or the sheer number of dark human souls that appeals to them. I don't know. What I do know is that they thrive on violence and mayhem and cannot be trusted."

Drumming his fingers impatiently on the table, Ptah said, "We don't need endless warnings. We need to find one...now."

Her tone took on a sharp edge. "Very well, Ptah. Most nights around midnight, they gather in the alleyway just outside of Bloodthirst. Most never come inside; however, there is one who is very bold, a demon of flames. She is pure evil and has been brave enough to approach the door, threatening to burn us. Many of the younger vampires were frightened away by her." Margarete narrowed her gaze and lowered her voice. "I'm quite certain she would be able to accomplish the task you need carried out."

Ptah rubbed his hands together eagerly. "It's just about party time now."

I gave him a look intended to remind him to take this seriously. "We're playing with fire...literally. You're too aloof about the whole situation, and we can't afford to make mistakes."

Amon echoed my words. "Beth is right, Ptah. We must be on our guard." He chuckled. "I'd hate to see you go up in smoke."

Ptah chuckled haughtily. "And I you, my friend."

"Look," I said, slamming my hand down on the table. "This isn't fun and games. It's dangerous. We have no idea what we're up against or how this demon will react to us. Get serious!"

Amon lost his amused smile. "Agreed."

Ptah did the same. "Agreed."

"All right," Margarete said, "Head over to the southeast corner of the building. Wait there at the entrance to the alley. She won't hesitate to approach you."

On our way out, we ran into Caleb and Philippe. Caleb gripped Philippe under his arms and propped him up against the wall. His head hung low, bobbing up and down like a puppet's. "The only way I could calm him down was to fill him with liquor," Caleb said with a shrug.

I stepped closer, lifted Philippe's head, and peered into his eyes. A drunken glaze greeted me. I threw a look over my shoulder at Caleb. "He's smashed and of no use to us. You should have left him at home."

"Look, Red," Caleb growled, stepping into my personal space. "I'm cleaning up *your* mess." His eyes darted back and forth between me and Amon. "This love triangle isn't working out...for anyone."

"We get that," Amon argued. "But your buddy here won't let go. Beth is just trying to appease him. We're all trying to appease him."

Ptah intervened. "Hey, now. This isn't the time nor the place for this conversation. Remember why we're here." He faced Caleb. "Margarete was helpful, pointing us in the direction of someone...or something... who can help. However, we don't have our witch. We must deal with a demon, a dangerous one of flames. We need our wits about us right now, so get it together or go back home."

Caleb took a step back, blinking. "A what?!"

"A demon of flames," Ptah calmly stated.

Caleb lifted a single eyebrow. "You've got to be joking."

Amon answered him. "It's no joke."

Caleb looked at me. "Beth?"

"It's true," I confirmed. "Witches won't cross Isis. Margarete said we needed someone, something more powerful."

His mouth fell slack, and he dropped his hands to his sides. "You're out of your friggin' minds. You can't believe anything a demon—" He stopped midsentence and looked to be deep in thought for a moment. "On second thought, I'm rather intrigued. I've never met a demon before." He grinned deviously before stating, "This may prove to be quite entertaining."

"Wonderful," Ptah responded. "But we must do something with Philippe. He's pretty much comatose."

Caleb grabbed Philippe's arm and wrapped it around his shoulder. "I'll bring him inside and have Margarete babysit. She owes me."

My gaze darted to Caleb. What reason could Margarete possibly have to be in his debt?

Caleb winked at me, then ducked inside the doors of Bloodthirst with Philippe. Moments later he returned and clapped his hands. "Are we ready, folks?"

"Be on your guard," Ptah warned. "And be ready for anything."

Amon grabbed my hand and pulled me a little closer as the four of us approached the southeast corner of the building. Once just inside the narrow alleyway, Caleb leaned against the wall, drumming his fingers on the concrete surface. Ptah stood alert, observing the night with rapid snaps of his head and his arms crossed. Amon angled his body slightly in front of mine, shielding me. I smothered a snicker. Inconspicuous we were not.

Off in the distance, at the far end of the alley, my vampire vision detected a faint orange glow. With a slow, steady gait it drifted closer, transforming into a feminine silhouette framed by saffron flames. The vibrant flashes of fire leapt and danced, stretching themselves out from her charcoal-colored flesh.

The thump of my heart crept up into my throat. I wanted to rush ahead of the others, greet her, blurt out our cause, beg for her help; yet I did nothing, remaining locked in place at the head of the narrow alleyway, watching nervously as she progressed toward us.

As she reached the corner of Bloodthirst, her ice-blue eyes regarded us suspiciously. "What do you want? Why do you stand before me?" she demanded as smoke seeped from between her charred lips.

Amon pushed me behind him, but it was Ptah who slowly approached the demon, holding his hands in front of him in a gesture of submission. With a quick jerk of her head, she focused on Ptah.

A trickle of perspiration formed on his brow. "Are you trying to set me ablaze?" Ptah challenged, sweeping a hand across his forehead. "I can call forth a layer of ice to shield my body before you could blink."

Twirling one of her ghost-white dreadlocks around a finger, she yawned before stating, "Vampire, I admire your courage to face me."

"Courage," Ptah retorted. "Do not test me demon. I am one of The Ten."

A wicked grin twisted her lips, and the flames surrounding her leapt with excitement. "And you need my help." It wasn't a question.

Amon was suddenly at Ptah's side, bellowing with laughter. "We do not require your assistance. We demand it."

Shrugging her shoulders, she stated flatly, "I do as I please."

"You *will* obey me, demon," Amon said, clenching his fists.

She sneered at him, lunging forward and striking Amon's face with her blazing hand. "I will not," she roared.

His flesh bubbled, then welted into an oozing blister. He raised a cooling hand to his cheek, stumbling backward to gawk at her in disbelief.

A frightened gasp escaped my throat.

She oozed arrogance, hands anchored to her hips, her chin held high. "Let that be a lesson for you."

Baring his fangs, Amon sucked in a chest full of air and exhaled mightily, blasting the demon against the side of the other building. Her luminous inferno flickered, and one by one her flames died away, revealing medieval metal armor that adorned her from head to toe. Without her cover of flames there was something hauntingly beautiful about her, like one of Danny's comic book characters come to life. I let out a small sigh and rubbed my hand over my heart. I hadn't thought about Danny in years. Strange how certain sights, sounds, or smells could trigger long-forgotten memories.

After his flawless complexion had been restored, Amon puffed himself up, boasting, "You may consider yourself to be very powerful, but nothing you could conjure would ever overshadow the magic which flows beneath my flesh. I am a god, and you are nothing more significant to me than a troublesome cloud of soot."

She glared at Amon and hissed, "Maybe, maybe not. Tell me what you want so I can be on my way."

"A locator spell," Ptah answered for him.

Her fiendish smile returned. "Spells are my passion. You should have mentioned this to begin with and spared us all the drama. Who are you looking for?"

Amon's expression went cold when he said, "Three members of The Ten: Osiris, Isis, and Hathor."

"They wronged you," she assumed.

"Yes."

Muscles in my face twitched. They wronged all of us. I couldn't just hide behind Amon and say nothing. I advanced a single step toward her.

Amon latched onto my arm, pulling me back. "Beth, no."

With a sweep of my hand, I brushed his away and faced her. It took several seconds to find my voice. "For five years I've suffered, my friends have suffered, as well as my husband. The three missing have been the cause of much pain. They must pay."

Caleb smirked. "Red, you've got nerve. Smokey doesn't seem to play nice."

The demon snapped her head in Caleb's direction; her flames reignited, but her glare was icy.

He raised his hands in surrender and backed away.

A wall of heat surged forward, rushing over me. My eyes watered and droplets of sweat laced my skin, but I held my stance and didn't look away.

Respect softened her face a touch. Her flames grew faint and then died away, as if someone had shut her off like a gas stove. "And they will pay," she assured me.

A desire to believe her words filled me, but Amon had rendered her flames useless with one breath, and even if she did indeed track down Osiris, Isis, and Hathor, infuriating three powerful vampire gods could mean her demise. Would she survive long enough to point out their location? "You seem very sure of yourself," I said, "but can you truly deliver them?"

Her ice-blue eyes glowed, and she answered with complete confidence, "Yes."

CHAPTER 6

O nce we arrived back home, I helped Philippe tumble into bed. His head hit the pillow and he moaned, rubbed his eyes, and then rolled over onto his side. I left him alone to sleep off the wine, proceeded downstairs, and joined the others in the foyer.

With his hands folded behind his back, Ptah paced the floor. "Again, we wait," he grumbled.

Caleb gave a half-hearted shrug. "It's not like we haven't done this before."

"It's different this time," I said. "Amon's back."

Erasing the distance between us, Amon scooted over to me and reached for my hands.

Ptah came to a stop. "This is true. We have much to be thankful for."

Caleb stretched his arms overhead and yawned. "We need some shut-eye, folks." He headed toward the front door but stopped abruptly and spun, pointing a finger at us. "Don't forget, The Gallery opens in three days. I expect all of you to be there." He added for good measure, "And dress to impress."

"I wouldn't miss it for the world." Ptah grinned and hooked his thumbs through his belt loops. "Planning on having Brit on my arm."

Amon bragged, "And I will have Beth on mine."

I stiffened just a bit. There was the whole business of Philippe's painting...*my* painting. I certainly couldn't show up on someone else's arm while obligated to support Philippe.

Caleb took a step toward us with a knowing look on his face. "Beth?"

I hesitated, scrambling for the right words. None came. "Well, I... it's complicated," I finally managed.

Amon frowned. "How so?"

"Philippe painted a portrait of Beth," Caleb offered up, enlightening him. "It's one of the pieces on display for opening night."

A sinking feeling started in my stomach, dropping all the way to my toes as I said, "For that reason, I feel my place is at Philippe's side."

Amon looked dazed for half a second. His eyes went cold. Clenching his jaw, he gave me a quick peck on the cheek, and with ice in his tone said, "Good night, Beth." Turning his back on me, he briskly walked out the front door.

"Amon," I called out, hurrying after him.

Ptah caught me, took my hands in his, and gave them a reassuring squeeze. "Let him go, Beth. I'll speak to him," he promised, then hurried off after his old friend.

Caleb sauntered across the foyer to stand at my side, and whispered in my ear, "You've just been dissed."

I rolled my eyes so hard they hurt and pointed to the door. "Go home, Caleb."

He trotted away, waving goodbye as he crossed the threshold with a smug grin.

I clenched my hands and then spread my fingers wide, releasing the tension in them. I needed a good, stiff drink. I journeyed eagerly toward the comforts of the study. My mouth watered as I stood before the doorway. I could almost taste the spicy flavor of what waited on the other side of the door for me, so much so it numbed my tongue. In my haste I pushed open the door and collided with Betty. When she tumbled backward, her hand flew to her chest and she gasped aloud. I seemed to keep running into her and knocking her down lately. I caught her before she could hit the floor and stood her upright. I called forth my most apologetic tone and said, "I am so sorry, Betty. I didn't expect to find anyone in here at this hour."

She clung to me, planting her feet in a wide, steady stance on the glossy floor. After a quick burst of high-pitched laughter, she released me and spoke in a low voice—though I knew neither of us was likely to rouse Philippe from his stupor. "I'm the one who should apologize, dear. I couldn't sleep and wandered over to pick out a book to read."

I wrapped my arm around her shoulders and pulled her farther into the room. "I was just going to pour myself a glass of brandy. Would you like one? It might help you sleep."

She gave me a kind smile. "Yes, I'd like that very much."

As we approached the bar, I gestured toward the high-backed chairs in front of the hearth. "Have a seat."

"Thank you," she said, settling into the one on the right. "I don't see much of you anymore." She looked unhappy about that. "But you look troubled, dear. What's on your mind?"

"Your timing couldn't be more perfect. Men," I said, and then shook my head in frustration. "I feel like a wishbone, being pulled apart in opposite directions."

"Amon and Philippe," she surmised.

Setting two snifters on the bar, I poured the brandy, filling each halfway. "Yes." I scooped up the glasses, moving to the hearth to sit opposite her. "If things weren't complicated enough before, Amon's return has exacerbated the situation."

She took a sip of brandy, grimaced, and then turned to face me. "May I be blunt?"

The stern look on her face told me I needed a good, healthy swallow of alcohol. I filled my mouth with the strong, hot liquor and let it slide down my throat. A tingle of pleasure scurried over my skin, making me shiver. This inspired another immediate sip. It burned on the way down, but in a comforting way, like strong sun on a summer day back when I'd been human. The impulse to close my eyes and savor the moment tempted me, but that would be rude. I owed her a response. Making direct eye contact, I answered, "Yes, please."

She set her glass on the hearth and folded her hands in her lap. "I believe you made up your mind the moment you realized Philippe wasn't your mysterious mist," she offered frankly. "Dragging out the inevitable and stringing along Philippe won't change what's in your heart."

My jaw dropped, and I fell backward into my chair. I'd never spoken of the mist to Betty. Where was this coming from? Had Philippe confided in her?

"You're wondering how I know," she said, interrupting my thoughts.

I nodded slowly.

"One drawback of running a household is the occasional, accidental intrusion upon private conversations." Her hands squirmed in her lap. "I overheard you and Caleb."

My mind raced backward, flipping through my memories. In moments, I knew which one she referred to: my dreaming of Amon, summoning Caleb, revealing my secret to him in the foyer, and then him rushing off to find answers. My focus returned to her. "All this time, and you never said a word."

"It wasn't my place," she replied, pursing her lips. "However, I certainly would like to scold Philippe. Learning what he'd done was very disappointing."

"Well, it's out in the open now," I pointed out.

"Maybe I should have spoken up back then." She sat a little taller. "At least I can offer my two cents now, for what it's worth."

I kept my eyes focused on her. "It's worth a great deal to me. I'm struggling with what to do. One day my heart goes left and the next day it goes right. What do I do?"

"Remaining by Philippe's side is only adding salt to the wound," she advised in a motherly tone. "I know you mean well, and you still care for him, but you love someone else. You only serve to offer Philippe false hope by staying."

"But he has begged me to work things out."

"*Are* you going to work things out?" she questioned.

Staring down at my hands lying limply in my lap, I took a deep painful breath and then quietly said, "I don't see how I can."

"Then you've answered your own question and prolonging it won't stop his pain or yours," she stated frankly. "Get it over with. Rip that bandage off."

I sank deeper into the chair, gathering the strength to acknowledge the truth. "You're right," I admitted. "But The Gallery opens in just a few days. I can't ruin the event for either Caleb or Philippe. I'll break things off with Philippe after the opening."

Betty rose from her chair and knelt down in front of me. Patting my hand, she said, "I'm proud of you, dear. Now go upstairs and get some rest."

I squeezed her hand. "Thank you, Betty."

"Good night," she said, picking up her book and moving toward the hallway.

"Good night."

****

The following evening, after strolling through Bloodthirst and fueling my eternal existence as a creature of the night, I rushed over to Ptah's to rectify things with Amon. With fresh, warm human blood running through my veins, the bitter chill of the night seeped into my bones. The winter wind howled and snatched up my scarf, tossing it over my shoulder as I stepped onto Ptah's porch.

Darkness lurked behind every window. Cocking my head, I listened with my heightened sense of hearing. No voices, heartbeats, or signs of life. I knocked anyway, focusing hard on the doorknob and willing it to turn from within. It failed to open to me, despite my efforts. Exhaling loudly, I hung my head, but my feet refused to walk away. Minutes sailed by before I gave in and turned to leave. I plopped down instead on the bottom step, sitting with my elbows on my knees and my chin in my hands. Where were they? More importantly, where was Amon? Was he avoiding me? I laughed out loud. *Impossible. So, go find him.* Springing to my feet, I trekked up the street in search of my missing love.

I wandered a short distance before stopping and scratching my head. I hadn't the faintest idea where to look. Philippe was right. I knew nothing of Amon's habits, the places he frequented, his hobbies, interests, or beliefs. We were complete strangers; yet, I loved him more than anything. But how could I love someone I knew nothing about? Did I love him just for the sake of loving him? For the sake of the familiarity built over the years with my ever-lingering mist? Did I love him because a binding ritual told me to?

My heartbeat slammed against my ribcage, and every breath struggled to escape my chest. *You're obsessing. Calm down.* I needed familiarity. Pressing my clammy hands into my temples, I scanned the street, searching for something, anything to take the edge off my emotions.

Off in the distance and inches from the cliffs, a bench caught my eye. Was it *the* bench, Danny's and mine? It couldn't be. That rickety old thing had to have crumbled to pieces years ago. Still, I clutched at my stomach and held my breath as my vampire eyesight zoomed in like a camera, pulling the image into focus. Releasing the paused breath, I uttered, "Plastic panels." Definitely not the bench from the past; yet, there it was, facing the ocean and beckoning me to sit and enjoy the view. I answered its call and hurried over, claiming my spot.

The glow of the moon cast a yellow hue over the tops of the trees. Its ribbons of lights coiled down the bark, spilling onto the brick walkway along the cliffs. Leaning back, I closed my eyes and let the white noise of the pounding surf clear my head.

The rhythmic sound of crashing waves created a soothing melody, gently easing all the tension with each whoosh and rumble. I sat upright and opened my eyes, gazing into the dead calm of the far horizon. A gust of wind nipped at my cheek. I pulled my scarf from around my neck and wrapped it snuggly about my head, blocking the bitter cold of the night air.

The tap of shoes scuffing along the sidewalk turned my head. A man and a woman strolled up the path, hidden beneath overcoats and hats. The man hummed playfully into the woman's ear. Giggling into her gloved hand, she hooked her arm through his and kissed his cheek.

The intoxicating scent of blood overwhelmed my senses, its metallic tang lingering in the air. Every fiber of my being longed to taste it, to savor its warmth on my tongue. However, my self-control was a delicate facade, and I fought against my primal instincts. I forced myself not to give into my desires. Giving them a polite nod, I dug my nails into my palms, letting them pass and sparing their lives.

Immediately behind them, a young woman dragged herself along the walkway, eyes cast downward as if she had nothing to live for. A dark peacoat and woven scarf protected her from the wind howling about the night. She paid no attention to the blustery weather, continuing on her path of misery. As she raised her head, an icy breath spilled from her cherry lips and hovered before her. I caught sight of her blue eyes, an exact replica of the ocean's hue. Something about her aura seemed ancient; yet, I couldn't place my finger on why.

As she neared me, her delicate fragrance perfumed the air, encircled me, and caught my attention. I'd never smelled the likes of such a soft scent. It seemed primitive, as if dried flowers and spices were grounded together by stone. As she lowered herself onto the bench, she let out a heartbreaking moan. She sat staring straight ahead, her arms dangling at her side. She appeared as though she hadn't a clue I was inches away from her.

As not to startle her, I spoke in a gentle tone. "Do you want to talk about it?"

Despite my efforts to be subtle, she jumped and jerked her head in my direction. Her chocolate-brown hair whipped at her cheek. She sharpened her gaze into a crystal clear glow, announcing that she, too, was a vampire.

"Don't be afraid," I assured her. "I mean you no harm. It's just you seem so...troubled. I thought you might need a shoulder to cry on." I extended my hand. "I'm Beth."

Uncertainty flickered in her ocean-blue eyes as she entwined a lock of hair around her slender finger. She seemed hesitant to take my hand. A burst of laughter escaped her cherry-red lips before she regained her composure. She held out her hand and said, "I am Hypatia."

I enclosed her pale fingers with mine. Her name seemed old and biblical in nature. Who was this sad female vampire sitting by my side?

Her pallid face suddenly beamed. She sat tall, swinging her legs back and forth under the bench. "I'm not sad, quite the opposite. Someone has touched my immortal heart and filled it with great joy."

"Really?"

"Yes," she replied. "Hours ago, I saved the life of a pregnant woman."

My mouth gaped, and I quickly snapped it shut. How refreshing, a vampire with a moral soul. "Then you saved two lives."

"You're right, I did; a baby boy." Her smile widened.

That sounded all too familiar, like my story, my past.

"You see." She turned to me, making sure she had my attention. "On a marvelous winter night many years ago, I was summoned by my father, demanding my presence and exclaiming a private matter required I come home at once. I knew the topic far too well. It became monotonous discussing day after day, year after year his money woes. I refused his request. Besides, I was applauding the extravagance of stringed instruments and couldn't be bothered."

It seemed important to her to unload her past, and on a perfect stranger no less. I guessed I fit the bill.

"When I did arrive on our doorstep, the delicate bouquet of forest trees towering around our home pulled me in their direction. Gazing at the brilliance of the twinkling stars gave me peace." Her brow twisted into a painful grimace. "My father, in a rage, barreled out of the house, coming straight at me and waving a sword. His breath reeked of liquor. I tried to get out of his way, but the sword moved in the same direction, slicing open my chest."

Ghastly as it was, why bare her soul to me? We were hardly connected. The itch to shrink away burned in my toes; yet, I sat still as if I hung on her every word.

"Of course, my father didn't intend to slay me. He held me in his arms, blubbering as I bled onto his clothes. It was my brother who saved me with his precious gift of life's blood." She spread her arms. "Turned me into the beautiful creature I am now."

Brushing my hands down my pants, I started to rise. "I should be—"

"I'm not finished," she snapped, her eyes wide and crazed.

I lowered myself back onto the bench, my eyes never leaving hers. *I'm sitting next to an insane vampire.*

"Where was I?" She squished her brows together in thought. The perplexed look lifted. "Oh, yes. I found my true love in this form. A kind, generous man who loved me dearly, so much so he gave up his human life to join mine." She looked to the ground, folding her hands and rest-ing them in her lap. "He was the only human I ever turned."

That statement got me. "What happened to him?"

She looked up at me, her eyes dark as the night. "My father set him on fire to punish me for creating a monster. My father believed in and worshipped God. There was no room in his life for evil, and the two of us, in his eyes, were the devil."

"I'm sorry," I whispered.

Her eyes brightened some. "Love as strong as ours doesn't die. It finds a way to return home, as did my true love's soul. He found a way back to me."

"How so?"

She spread her lips into a knowing grin. "The unborn child."

I edged closer. "Yes."

"My lover's soul is inside the baby."

I bolted upright and took a step back. *Okay, she flipped the crazy switch.* "You can't be serious. How is that even possible?"

Lifting her hands and shaking her head, she said, "I don't know, but I can feel him inside the mother's womb...his love, I mean."

I knew love like that, that powerful feeling that grips you so hard you can't breathe. I fell in love with mist. How could I criticize her? I returned to my seat, sitting closer to her. "What are you going to do?"

"I will wait for him to mature, and when he begins to experience craving, a craving he cannot understand, I will ask him to share our immortal world."

"You can't interfere like that. He no longer belongs to you. Think about the boy's life."

Rage blemished her beautiful face and angry tears stained her cheeks. "But I have the power to change that. I can ease his suffering."

"You're talking about a child who hasn't even been born," I warned, trying to reason with her.

A slew of heart wrenching tears flooded from her eyes. "Of that I'm well aware."

I cradled her in my arms, speaking softly to her, "Hypatia, if it's meant to be, the boy will find you. Until then, there is nothing you can do."

"Run along now, Hypatia," Amon said, his voice coming up from behind.

I turned and found him standing inches from the bench. I regarded him with narrowed eyes. How did he know her? "She just wants to talk," I said, glancing toward her. The bench was completely empty, and she was long gone. I turned back to Amon. "So you know her?"

"Our paths have crossed through acquaintances."

"She seems very troubled."

"And then some," he revealed. "She wanders the world, searching for the ghost of her dead vampire lover."

"Well...according to her, she's found him."

"Indeed! She's claimed that time and time again. Thinks his soul is locked inside a human. Kohath is beside himself with worry."

"Kohath?" I questioned.

He nodded. "Hypatia is his sister. He turned her."

I blinked and widened my eyes. *The story she told me was about Kohath?* I let out a stunned, "What?!"

Amon forced a laugh. "I could go now, but I came to see you."

"I just came from Ptah's looking for you, too. How did you know where I'd be?"

He shoved his hands into his pockets and heaved his shoulders in an upward motion. "I use my blood, which flows inside you."

I pressed my lips flat and stared in disbelief. *What the hell?*

He bobbed his head toward the bench. "May I sit?"

I scooted over. "Please."

He sat down, pressing his fingers together to form a tent. "The simplest way to explain...it's like GPS. My blood tracks you. That's how I found you at Ptah's gala."

I sat with my mouth hanging open. You track a car, or a criminal, or a dog, but not a lover. "You're saying that, at any given time, you know where I am?" I angled my body away from him. "I have no privacy!"

He slid closer, so close our legs touched. Stroking my cheek, he said softly, "I cherish you, hold you dear to my heart. Going after Osiris, Isis, and Hathor is a dangerous endeavor. I want to protect you. Keep you safe. That's why I use my gift, not to spy on you."

Tucking my hand inside his coat pocket, I leaned into him. "My knight in shining armor."

He kissed the top of my head. "Indeed." He held me tight. "I wanted to apologize for rushing off last night. It was inconsiderate. Forgive me?"

I snuggled even closer. "You're forgiven." I met his eyes. "I came to tell you that I've made a decision."

He studied every inch of my face. "And?"

"After The Gallery's opening, I'm going to tell Philippe it's over."

He brought my hand to his lips and kissed it. "I know this wasn't an easy decision for you."

I shook my head. "No, it wasn't, but it's the right decision, and you and I have a long road ahead of us. We have a lot to learn about each other, and I don't want there to be secrets."

He flinched slightly. "Secrets...what secrets?"

"I don't know. I just—I mean, my relationships haven't exactly worked out." I wrapped my hand around his forearm. "More than anything, I want us to be happy."

He leaned forward, touching his lips to my ear. "We will be." His soft lips brushed across my cheek, finding my mouth. Blood pumped intense hunger through my veins. In his arms, I went limp, like a rag doll. *Take me. Do what you will.* His fingers surrounded the swell of my breast, fondling, searching, teasing. My skin ached with need. I trembled, moaned, and begged to be taken.

Philippe's voice slammed inside my brain. *Beth, we need to talk.*

I scrambled to my feet. My gaze darted in every direction, searching for him.

Amon hurried after me, claiming my arm. "Beth, what is it? What's wrong?"

Philippe's voice filled my head again. *This can't wait. Come home.*

His message was verbal, and only inside my head. I slouched forward in annoyance. "He's not here."

Amon took me by the shoulders and forced me to face him. "Who's not here? You're not making sense."

"Philippe. I thought he was here, watching us, but he only reached out to me in thought. I'm being paranoid."

He chuckled. "Maybe a little."

I drew in a breath, holding onto it as if it were my last, before blowing it all out in one gasp. "I just need all of this to be over."

His eyes grew bright and glossy. In a soothing tone, he said, "Just a few more days and it will be." He held out his hand. "Come, I have something to show you."

"Philippe wants me to come home." My tone lacked enthusiasm. The night was young, and I intended to play a while longer.

He smirked. "Does he?"

"Yes," I said, giggling behind my hand.

"Then, we should get going if I'm going to have you home in good time."

"And where are we going?"

"You'll see." He slipped his arm around my waist. "It's not far, just up the street."

"What are you up to?" I queried, suspicious. "The only thing up the street is Sea Cliff Towers."

He kissed the tip of my nose. "Ah, now you've ruined my surprise."

"I don't get it. What surprise?"

He gave me a playful nudge. "Guess."

I nudged him back. "No."

Sweeping me up into his arms, he whisked me off into the night sky, soaring like a jet straight for the Towers. Speed and wind imprisoned my arms and legs, pinning me happily against Amon's body. A vacuum of wind sucked up my scarf, ripping it from my head. Amon caught the tail end of it just before it spiraled off into space. He tucked it into my jacket without missing a beat and sheltered my face inside his coat. The spicy-sandalwood scent of his cologne made every nerve stand at attention. Parting my lips, I ran my tongue up his neck and nibbled on his ear.

He shivered and laughed. "Stop, you'll make me crash."

Smashing my nose against his neck and inhaling deeply, I whispered, "I could just gobble you up."

"Hold that thought. We're here."

In a gradual descent, we floated like feathers, landing delicately on the ground in front of The Sea Cliff Towers. I strained my neck to peer all the way to the top of the hexagon-shaped high-rise. Grayish clouds hovered above the roof, blocking out the sheen of the moon.

The whoosh of doors swinging open claimed my attention. A doorman clad in a dark suit and hat approached us. "Good evening, Amon. Welcome back," he said, holding open the doors.

I looked from the doorman to Amon. What was he up to?

"Thank you, Jacob. May I take another look?" Amon asked, placing his hand on the small of my back and leading me inside.

The doorman, Jacob, escorted us across the travertine floor toward a gold-faced elevator and pushed the call button. "Your agent left the key with me. I'll bring you up and let you in."

Amon glanced at me, beaming. "I'm hoping it will take her breath away."

Was this his surprise, a home?

The elevator chimed right before the doors parted. With a roll of his hand, Jacob said, "After you."

Amon and I entered, hand in hand. Jacob faced a panel box and slipped in a key card. *Penthouse* flashed on the digital monitor. The elevator whined, jumped, and then hummed to life, climbing higher and higher, whizzing past every floor. Spending every waking minute of every day for the rest of our immortal lives was what I'd dreamt about my entire human life—and for the past five years. It wasn't just a dream anymore. I watched in disbelief as the numbers increased on the monitor, *30…31…32…33…34…Penthouse.* The elevator rolled to a leisurely stop. The doors slid open, like a curtain revealing the set at a theater. Our act one was a hand-carved wooden door with an oversized wrought-iron handle.

"Come," Jacob said, ushering Amon and I into the marble hallway. Digging into his coat pocket, he pulled out a bulky silver key, slipped it into the lock, and swung the door inside. "Take as much time as you need. I'll wait out here."

"Thank you," Amon told him before leading me through the massive doorway. A dark marble staircase leading to the second floor monopolized the front entrance. Maple-colored hardwood floors stretched the entire length of the unit. Beveled windows nestled in every corner created a bird's-eye view of the twinkling city below.

"I don't know where to look first," I breathed in complete amazement.

A satisfied smile came to his lips. "Let me take you on a tour." He pulled me along into the ultra-modern kitchen with dark cabinets and stainless-steel appliances. "A chef's dream kitchen." He winked at me. "Something of no interest to us, but..." He skated over to the massive refrigerator and opened one door wide. "This baby can hold a lot of blood."

I gave him a thumbs up. "No doubt."

Waving me over, he said, "There's more to see."

With excitement like a child on Christmas morning, he bounced from room to room, dragging me along with him. As we explored each one, I grew dizzy with disbelief. Repeatedly, I exclaimed, "Oh, my gosh!" The two-story unit, complete with three bedrooms, four bathrooms, 360-degree views on each floor, and three balconies—our home perched up in the sky—was absolutely perfect.

At the end of his tour, when we'd arrived back at the front door, he fairly shrieked, "Do you like my surprise?"

"Like?" I blurted out. "Are you kidding? I love it."

He swept me up in his arms and swung me around. Setting me on my feet, he held me at arm's length while he appraised my eyes. "Should I put in an offer?"

Rising up on my toes, I embraced him. "Yes."

CHAPTER 7

Just after midnight I strolled up the porch steps, humming. I plopped down on the first step, stretching my arms overhead. All was right with the world, though our circumstances hadn't changed. Amon wanted vengeance. Osiris, Isis, and Hathor remained hidden. Philippe wanted to work things out, and I wanted my freedom—but none of that mattered. Amon loved me, and I loved him. With him at my side, I could conquer anything.

The front door flew open, and Philippe stepped onto the porch. "What are you doing out here? Come inside."

My heart pounded with defiance as I slammed the door behind me and marched into the foyer.

He crossed his arms and narrowed his eyes. "Where have you been?"

My hands clenched briefly. "Lots of places, but that's not really what you want to know, is it?"

He forced out a laugh. "You're right. Were you with *him*?"

I let out a groan as my gaze flicked heavenward. "You can't even say his name now?"

He spit out between clenched teeth...and fangs, "Were...you...with... Amon?"

I held my chin high in defiance. "Yes."

"Did you even come home last night? I wouldn't know, seeing as how *someone* drugged me," Philippe accused as his eyes narrowed

"Of course, I did. I changed your clothes, got you into bed, and stayed with you." I jutted a rigid finger at him. "Caleb was the one who filled you with liquor."

He stood there, trembling, his eyes shifting back and forth, his forehead wrinkling in remorse. He cleared his throat. "I'm sorry. I didn't know."

I sighed. "All we do is argue. It's exhausting."

He bowed his head and nodded. "You're right." His voice seemed to lose all its power. "I don't even know how to act around you anymore."

Just tell him. Get it over with. I bit my bottom lip. The Gallery's opening was three days away. Clamping my mouth shut, I shoved the words back down my throat like bitter medicine.

His posture sagged and he turned to face the stairs. "It's been a long evening. I'm going to turn in. Good night."

My eyes followed him as he vanished down the second-floor hallway. Placing my hands on my hips, I stared at the empty stairway. *What the hell was that?* One minute he demanded answers, and the next he stormed off. Tilting my head back and staring at the ceiling, I let out a loud, long groan. Sleeping in our bed was out of the question. The bickering would only continue. We both needed space. Once again, I'd turn down the sheets in the white room.

I climbed the stairs two at a time but hesitated at the top. I glanced at our bedroom door, which stood ajar. *Damn it.* I had to pass it to get to the white room. Had he left it open on purpose, hoping I'd join him? I slipped out of my shoes and tiptoed down the hallway, not daring to breathe as I inched past our door. The rustling of sheets played at full volume in my left ear. I bolted, ducking inside the white room and sealing the door shut. Exhaling, I leaned against the frame and wiped my brow. I didn't move. I stood with my ear to the door, listening. Dead silence. I blew out a couple of relieved breaths before pushing away from the door. Fumbling out of my clothes, I flopped down on the bed and closed my eyes. Visions of Amon danced within my brain. I melted into the mattress and drifted off.

My stomach growled, waking me from sleep. *Damn hunger.* I kicked off the covers and struggled to get out of bed.

Beth. Amon's heavenly voice entered my head. *Join me at Ptah's for a warm glass of blood.*

I bolted straight up then. *Love to.* Leaping off the bed, I dashed into the bathroom to grab a hurried shower. Wrapped in a towel, I hurried down the hall toward our room. An image of Philippe, arms crossed and eyes ablaze, demanding to know where I was off to, plagued my imagination. I mulled over excuse after excuse but couldn't come up with anything that might appease Philippe.

I bit the bullet, twisted the doorknob, and pushed the door open. With my head held high, I entered with the poise of a queen. Honesty was the best policy, right? "Philippe, I'm off to see Amon."

No response.

The bedroom was still and lifeless. No rustling of sheets, no water tapping against the bottom of the tub, no hangers smacking the back wall of the closet as clothing was pulled free. I approached the bed and pulled back the curtain. A beautifully made bed with every pillow in its proper place came into view. I let the drapes fall and turned toward the doorway. He'd left the house without a word. I sat on the edge of the bed, puzzled. It wasn't like him. In fact, it was more like me.

I popped up off the bed. *Whatever.* Amon was waiting, and Philippe's early departure saved me a repeat of last night's bickering. I let the towel drop to the floor and ransacked my closet. I slipped into black-lace panties and matching bra, a sheer blouse, acid-washed jeans, and black boots. I put on a dark coat, threw my hair over my shoulder, and stepped out the door feeling confident and stylish.

The crisp night air stung my cheeks before I flipped my coat collar upward and hid behind the thick wool. As I gracefully soared into the starlit sky, the world beneath me grew smaller and smaller as I glided effortlessly through the inky darkness. In a matter of minutes, I arrived at Ptah's house. The door flew wide open before I could even lift my fist to knock.

Amon darted through the door, pulling me into his arms and pressing his soft lips to mine. "I couldn't wait to see you," he said between kisses.

The air around me grew fuzzy. There was only Amon. Laughing, I threw my arms around his neck, rose onto my toes, and nuzzled at his ear.

"Let the poor girl in," Ptah said, coming up behind Amon, his hands on his hips.

"Come in," Amon said, taking my hand and leading me inside.

I acknowledged Ptah briefly before losing myself in Amon's emerald-green eyes. Our gazes locked on each other as we glided into the front room.

"A toast. To immortality," Ptah said, sprouting a wicked grin as he handed us glasses of blood from the coffee table.

"To immortality." Amon clinked his glass to mine and tilted his head back to take a generous swallow.

I followed his lead, stroking my throat as the ambrosia became a part of me. I didn't know which pleased me more, blood or sex.

Amon winked at me.

Heat rushed to my cheeks. *Definitely sex.*

After knocking back the contents of his own glass, Ptah abandoned it on the coffee table and grabbed his coat from the back of the chair. "Well, I'm off to Brit's." He waggled a finger at us. "Behave."

Hooking an arm around Amon's shoulder, I replied, "Not a chance."

Amon waved goodbye eagerly. "Go on. Get out of here and give Brit our love."

"Will do." Ptah backed out of the room, leaving us alone. Seconds later, the front door settled into its frame, closing off the night.

Amon frowned slightly as he led me to the sofa. "I know Philippe is filling your head with doubts about us." He tucked a strand of hair behind my ear. "It doesn't matter if you know my favorite color is black, or that I sit by the ocean to gather my thoughts, or that I have a passion for the arts, or that my arrogance gets me into trouble time and time again...none of that matters. My heartbeat is your heartbeat, my breath is your breath, and my soul is your soul, right?"

I touched my fingertips to my lips. Tears moistened my eyes. "Yes," I whispered.

"That's all that matters."

I swiped at my eyes, snuggling closer. I leaned into him, listening to the peaceful rhythm of his immortal heart keeping perfect time within his chest.

"Let's go have some fun," he suggested, pulling me to my feet. Reaching into his coat, he smiled secretively. "Guess what I have in my pocket?"

"Tickets." Wasn't that usually the surprise men kept hidden inside their coat pockets, other than a ring?

He deliberately raised his brow. "But to what?"

I glanced at his coat, then at him, waiting for some nonexistent clue to materialize. I finally shrugged in defeat. "I have no idea."

He produced the rectangular pieces of paper and laid them in my lap. "The Performing Arts Festival at the cliffs. So close, it's almost in Ptah's backyard."

"I've never been."

"You'll love it. But let's be off. We only have about ten minutes to get to our seats." He winked at me. "Of course, I can get us there in one."

By the time we arrived, the open-air theater was overflowing with buzzing spectators. Stars flickered throughout the raven sky, playing hide-and-seek with the gleaming moon. A gentle ocean breeze stirred up the mixture of floral perfume, musky cologne, and a potpourri of human blood. I took a generous whiff and licked my lips. Amon rested his hand on the small of my back and murmured, "Heavenly, isn't it?"

"Very."

He kissed me right then and there. I sank into his embrace and could have stayed that way forever, but he broke our kiss to lead me down to the second level. Amon halted at the fifth row, and we inched down the aisle, stopping midpoint. "Here we are."

We settled into our seats just as the lights dimmed on the half-moon stage. Conversations grew hushed, then died away.

Crashing waves mimicked muted applause as the deep-lavender velvet drapes surrounding the stage parted.

"They're starting," a voice in the crowd blurted out.

Scooting to the edge of my seat, I peered down at the stage. Life-like statues with frozen smiles and clasped hands stood on display, like a department store. I studied them from every angle. There was something extraordinarily human about them—the tilt of their heads, the loneliness in their eyes...and the blood coursing through their veins. *Blood!*

Suddenly, they moved, scattering to all corners of the stage, merging limbs and locking hands, forming mountain peaks with a touch of white snow with their bodies.

Touching Amon's arm, I uttered, "They're human."

He didn't say a word, just pressed his fingers more firmly around my hand.

I held my breath each time the curtain closed and gasped as it reopened, unveiling yet another enchanting scene. Actors glided across the stage, transforming into birds spreading their wings in flight. Raindrops expanded into lakes and ink silhouettes blossomed into colorful butterflies. Brilliant olive-green leaves sprouted magically upon naked trees. The world around me drifted away, my mind erasing everything and everyone except the performance. Never in my life had I witnessed such creativity, such raw emotion. The drapes parted for the last time. The actors, standing in a long line of clasped hands, took a bow. The audience roared to life.

Springing to my feet, I called out as loud as I could, "Bravo, bravo!"

"I was worried you wouldn't take a breath for the duration of the performance."

I hugged Amon close. "Thank you for bringing me. It was such a moving experience. I couldn't take my eyes off them."

"I chose wisely then. You feel better, yes?"

I couldn't help but smile. "Yes."

****

That night I crawled into the bed Philippe and I shared, alone. Philippe kept to himself, sulking about the house and avoiding me. Tomorrow The Gallery would open. When I rolled over and fluffed the pillow, my wedding ring caught the moonlight streaming in from the parted drapes on the west side of the bed. I frowned as I twisted it back and forth around my finger. I didn't even know if Philippe wanted me here. Did he already know what I'd decided? Maybe that was the reason for his distance. Had he given up? Was he finally ready to set me free? Sinking into my pillows, I let go of my ring and let my hands fall against the mattress. I could play the maybe game all night and still be none the wiser. Instead, I closed my eyes, allowing my thoughts to drift to Amon. My breathing slowed, and drowsiness inched over my entire body.

The potent smell of blood sank its teeth in and yanked me from sleep. I bolted upright, rubbing my eyes and gazing at...Philippe? He stood there, waving a mug of blood under my nose. Wobbling on his feet and sloshing blood against the sides of the mug, he leaned over me, wine tainting his breath. "Wake up, my porcelain doll."

I climbed from bed and took the mug, setting it on the night table. "Are you drunk?"

A black tie hung slack around his neck on top of his unbuttoned white shirt. Pinching his thumb and index finger together, he grinned mischievously. "A little."

I shook my head at him. "Philippe, The Gallery opens tonight. You can't show up drunk."

He threw a hand in the air. "Why not? This is Caleb's shindig. I'm just along for the ride." He pointed a finger at me. "And to sell that damn painting of you."

My mouth opened, but there were no words waiting to be spoken.

Bobbing his head toward the mug, he said, "Drink your blood."

I glanced at the mug and then at him, frowning. We'd never kept blood in the house. "Where did you get the blood?"

As he attempted to button his shirt, he shrugged halfheartedly. "I've got a human tied up in one of the rooms upstairs."

I shuffled back a few steps and bumped up against the bed frame. "What?!"

He burst out laughing. "I'm kidding. Come on, Beth, did you really think I was serious? Ptah gave me a couple of bags. If you don't believe me, check the fridge."

Unable to move, I stood there, not knowing what to say. Finally, I gained my composure and spoke. "That's not even funny. Why would you joke about something like that? What is wrong with you?"

He ignored my questions and tilted his head toward the bathroom. "Grab a shower. Change. I don't want to be late." He snapped his fingers. "Oh yeah, I almost forgot. I bought you a dress." He staggered into the closet, rustling through our clothes until he found a black dress, which he slipped off its hanger. Holding it up in front of him, he said, "It's Ralph Lauren. Do you like?"

The elegant off-the-shoulder gown looked like he'd snatched it right off a New York runaway. He laid the dress on the bed, picking up the mug and placing it in my hands. "Drink up. We've got to get going."

I held up the mug. "What about you? Have you fed?"

He scowled. "Yes, yes; now go on. Get ready."

Without a second thought, I downed the mug's contents, licked the residue from my lips, and set the empty mug on the nightstand. Picking up the dress, I took a couple of hesitant steps toward the bathroom, stopped, and turned to Philippe. He stood in front of the floor-length mirror, whistling while knotting his tie. How did one flip the switch from brooding to whistling cheerily? Perhaps it was too much wine or maybe the excitement of the opening, but for whatever reason, something was off.

He caught me staring and tapped his wrist, though I'd never seen him wear a watch. "Time's ticking away, Beth."

I lingered a moment longer before turning my back on him and entering the bathroom. Within twenty minutes I'd showered, changed, and knotted my hair into a loose bun. I spun in a circle, showing off the new dress, when I reentered the room. "Ready."

Light danced in his eyes as they traveled over my body, taking in every inch. He wagged his finger at me in an exaggerated fashion. "I knew that dress was you. You're a vision of absolute loveliness." He extended his arm. "Jon Paul's waiting."

I straightened his tie before hooking my arm through his. "And you look very handsome."

He winked at me. "Let's go have some fun."

Stuffing the dreadful task of telling him we were over deep inside my black chest, I forced a smile and let him lead me down the stairs and out the front door to where Jon Paul was waiting.

"To The Gallery, Mr. Delon?"

"Yes, thank you," Philippe answered as he slid in beside me.

On the short car ride over, neither of us spoke. It wasn't an awkward silence; rather, more like we were at ease with one another. Philippe sat close, lacing our fingers and resting our hands on my thigh like old times. Was he trying to recreate part of our past? Maybe, or maybe he was merely hoping for a future. Past or future, neither mattered. We weren't the same two people. Too much had changed between us, and not for the better. We weren't meant to be...too many obstacles in the way. We'd knock one down and another would appear. Philippe's deception and my love for Amon had mounted to the point they couldn't be ignored. At the end of the night, I would admit defeat and let him go.

Jon Paul parked in front of The Gallery, and Philippe climbed out, offering me his hand. "Are you ready to stand in the spotlight?"

"You're referring to the painting, I presume."

He nodded slightly. "I'm a little jealous. Someone is going to take you home tonight and hang you on their wall." He grew quiet, his face less animated.

I gave his hand a squeeze. "If you don't want to sell it, then don't."

His face brightened. "Maybe I won't. We'll see. Jon Paul, I'm not sure how long we'll be. I'll call you when we're ready."

"Yes, Mr. Delon."

Philippe escorted me through the massive glass door of The Gallery, and I couldn't help but stare at Caleb's bizarre theme dotting the entirety of the narrow room. Works of art adorned the polished walls like miniature backdrops leading to alternate realms, suspended above twisted sculptures of stone and marble standing tall and proud upon the hardwood floor. In Philippe's ear, I whispered, "It's magnificent."

"Caleb's a perfectionist. He had to get it right," he whispered back. He ambled in front of me and took both my hands. "Come, let's revisit my painting."

He didn't wait for my reply. Ducking behind me and sliding around to my side, he led me to the center wall of the room. There I was, plastered larger than life on the wall for all to see.

A mixed crowd of humans and vampires gathered around us, gawking and pointing at it; at *me!* A man with unbelievably broad shoulders touched the arm of the woman standing next to him. "The artist captured her beauty brilliantly."

A woman standing next to him lifted her hand and traced the frame. "The emotion in the painting is almost haunting."

A male vampire lightly touched the bottom of the canvas. "The brush strokes speak to his passion."

Philippe let go of me and thrust himself into the midst of their conversation. "Why, thank you."

All eyes turned to him and then darted to me, transfixed. Too many eyes scrutinized every detail of my face. "Bravo, Bravo!" they all yelled simultaneously, their eyes widening.

A male among them shouted, "Is she your muse?"

Philippe's lips adopted a devil-may-care grin. "She is."

Oh, for the love of god. I wanted to die.

"Whatever you're asking, I'll double it." Amon's voice overshadowed all the others.

His voice called forth visions of red rose petals falling inside my brain. I could almost feel them cascade over me, caressing the entire surface of my skin. I shuddered and brushed my hands over my arms. I found his emerald-green eyes within the crowd. The sight of him, dressed in a classic black suit and wearing his hair neatly slicked back into a smooth ponytail, quickly accelerated my heart rate.

Amon launched himself across the room, stopping short once he stood before me. Yearning filled his eyes as they traveled over my face and down the length of my body. A rosy glow suffused his cheeks. "I can't take my eyes off you. You look exceptionally mesmerizing, my love."

I reached out to touch his arm. "And you look...dashing."

"I must have this painting," he said, in a low, serious tone. "The likeness is perfect."

"It's not for sale," Philippe said in a scathing tone.

My gaze darted to Philippe. I'd completely forgotten he was there.

Amon raised his eyebrows and gave Philippe a glassy stare. "Does that apply to everyone or only to me?"

Philippe pressed his lips flat. "Not for sale means not for sale."

Stepping between them, I laid my hand on Philippe's chest. "It's okay. Relax."

A cold glaze darkened his eyes, and with both hands he shoved me backward into Amon.

Amon's mouth fell open as I fell into his arms. After he steadied me, he jerked his head toward Philippe. "What the hell is wrong with you?"

But Philippe was focused on me. From between clenched teeth his words flew at me. "You don't give a shit about me or how I feel." His lips twitched and curled upward. "I can't stand the sight of you." Turning his back on me, he plowed his way over to the far corner of the room.

Everyone gathered around the painting stood motionless, with their eyes wide and their lips clamped shut. One by one they broke free and scattered away from Amon and me.

"I need some air."

Lightly stroking my forearm, Amon said, "There's a park across the street. We can go there."

Hiding my face with my hand, I said, "Yes, wherever, just get me out of here."

Like a bodyguard, Amon held me close and rushed me out the front door of The Gallery. We hurriedly cut through the maze of lofty pine trees concealing the park. Fresh cut grass and pine needles co-mingling their scents flavored the air.

"There's a bench up ahead." Amon guided me toward it. "We can sit for a while and clear our heads."

I reached for his hand. "That sounds wonderful."

Hand in hand we drifted up the slate-brick walkway, as if we didn't have a care in the world. Amon pulled me down on the bench next to him. "This is a lovely spot."

I glanced about us before answering. "It's serene." I nudged at his shoulder. "Thank you for rescuing me."

He wrapped his arms around the back of the bench. "What can I say? I can't resist a damsel in distress." As an afterthought, he removed his jacket, wrapping it around my exposed shoulders. "There's a chill in the air, my lady."

"Thank you, kind sir."

We laughed at each other, leaning back into the bench.

"Do you feel better?" he asked, running a finger along my cheek.

I stroked my fingers across the back of his hand. "Much."

Over his shoulder I caught the gleam of moonlight on the metal surface of a slide in the distance. Rising to my feet and standing on my tiptoes, I could make out a full-service playground beyond the edge of the trees. I giggled and pulled Amon to his feet. "Come, we can be children again."

Puzzlement creased his brow. "Beth, you do realize I was never a child?"

"Humor me," I said, pointing. "Look. There's a playground full of fun things we can do. Let's go play."

His gaze wandered in its direction before returning to me. "Must we?"

I coaxed him forward. "Yes, we must."

When we reached the edge of the circular, sandy-floored playground, he shook his head. "I don't get it."

My eyes roamed over the swing set, jungle gym, slide, teeter-totter, and merry-go-round. Thrusting my arms upward into a V, I shouted, "Score."

He offered me a bemused smile.

I ignored him, running to the swing set and planting myself in one of the swings. "Push me."

With a slow, reluctant gait he approached. "This is ridiculous, Beth. You're a vampire of five years, and I'm centuries old. We don't play on playgrounds."

"You're being a fuddy-duddy."

He bellowed with laughter. "A what?"

"Never mind. Just get over here and push me."

He obliged halfheartedly.

I turned in the swing and glared at him in displeasure.

"Fine."

The next push threw me high into the air, and I squealed with delight. "Higher," I commanded.

He obeyed. As I skyrocketed upward, I gazed into the sparkling sky. The cool night air tossed my hair.

Amon stepped in front of me, grabbing the chains and forcing me to a halt. "This thing is bouncing off the ground. If it comes unhinged, we're going to ruin it for the kids who actually play here."

"We wouldn't want to do that now, would we?" I hopped off and dashed over to the merry-go-round. I waved him over. "Let's try this next."

He placed his hands on his hips and huffed out, "What is this, a poor man's carousel? They expect you to push it?"

I couldn't help but smile. He was definitely out of his element. "You get on one side, and I get on the other. We start running as fast as we can and then jump on."

"You can't be serious! It will spiral up into the stratosphere if I run at full speed."

"Human speed, silly."

Furrowing his brows, he shook his head. "Why would I want to get on something that spins me around? It sounds like a waste of time."

I tried to come up with a comparison he might be familiar with. "It's fun, like the teacups at Disneyland."

The crease on his forehead deepened and he threw his hands up. "I haven't a clue what teacups at Disneyland is."

I rolled my eyes, and then put force behind my voice. "You're impossible. Get on that side and start running...but slowly."

He gripped the rail and broke into a brisk walk, nearly knocking me off my feet. Even running I could barely keep up with him. Soon the merry-go-round was spinning at top speed.

"Jump on," I shouted, lurching onto the platform and clinging to the nearest post. Amon hopped on the opposite side, latching on to his own post. The merry-go-round whirled round and round, gathering speed. The gears screeched, and its undercarriage rumbled like an earthquake. Tears flew from my eyes and the force of the wind ripped through my hair, unwinding my bun. We both screamed with all the force in our lungs. I swore it might really launch us into space as Amon had joked about earlier. But eventually the gears grew quiet, the rumbling died down, and we gradually slowed. I let go and tumbled across the ground, sprawling my arms and legs like I was making snow angels once I'd come to a stop. Amon wobbled over on his hands and knees to collapse beside me.

Stars swirled together and the world had turned upside down. I couldn't focus, even bringing my preternatural vision into play. "Everything is spinning."

"Look up at the stars, Beth. They look more like shooting comets."

Squeezing my eyes shut, I swallowed hard. "I can't. I feel sick."

He scooted closer to me and laid his hand on my stomach. "Listen to my voice and breathe slowly in and out."

I did until the earth came to a standstill, and I could open my eyes to find the air and objects around me at peace.

"Better?"

"Yes." He stared down at me with his striking emerald-green eyes, making me feel weak. Sitting up and turning away, I said, "We should get back."

Amon rose and brushed sand from his clothes before offering me his hand. "I'll go first, and then you follow."

"Yes, that works."

He kissed me softly, and then I watched him walk away. I situated myself on the edge of the merry-go-round, unwilling as of yet to go back inside and face Philippe. Me running off with Amon certainly must have pressed all his buttons; buttons it was becoming increasingly difficult to switch off. Maybe a note would be better. *Dear Philippe, Regrettably, I must tell you goodbye.* A moment later I was chastising myself. *Regrettably...really? Is that the best you can do?* I bit my lip hard. A note was out of the question. It was cruel, cold, and way too impersonal. No, I had to suck it up and find the courage to tell him to his face. Slumping forward, I let my head fall into my hands. I didn't know how to do it. I'd never broken up with anyone before. Danny had been the one to walk away from me, with very few words spoken to mark the occasion.

I sat there for some time, staring out into the night, my mind a blank while growing no closer to an answer. Hesitantly I got to my feet. My hands trembled, and I had to force each step forward. I eyed The Gallery nervously from across the street once I'd cleared the park. It took another several minutes for me to be capable of moving from this new spot. But in the next instant, with vampire speed, I stood in front of the glass door, my hand gripping the latch. Steeling myself for the task at hand, I swung the door open and walked inside with my chin held high.

The room had cleared so that it no longer appeared to contain a solid wall of bodies. Browsing the faces in the remaining crowd, I spotted Ptah, dressed sharply in a fitted tan suit, engaging in conversation with a man covered in tattoos as they took turns gesturing in the direction of a marble sculpture. Brit posed next to him, resting her hand on her hip, seductive in her black cocktail dress which plunged to racy depths in both the front and the back. He inclined his head at me in acknowl-edgement. I waved quickly before continuing my search for Philippe.

For the first time that night I ran into Caleb, debonair in his expensive pale-gray suit. A tall, slender girl was hooked on his arm, turning heads in her backless, burgundy-colored dress that hugged her body like a second skin. She turned her head to the side, and I did a double take. No, it couldn't be. I boldly walked up to them and tapped her on the shoulder. She turned, revealing familiar violet-colored eyes.

"Hello, Beth," Margarete said, tossing her hair over her shoulder. Brushing sand from my hair, she snickered. "Where've you been?"

"A playground." The word fell from my mouth absentmindedly.

Caleb barked out laughter. "A children's playground?"

I ignored him completely. "What are you doing here...and with Caleb?"

Caleb rested his hand on the small of her back. "She's my date."

My gaze flicked back and forth several times between the pair. "I didn't know...since when? You're dating?"

They exchanged a look of great familiarity. Margarete laughed delicately and Caleb beamed. "I've known Margarete a long time. We have a...special relationship."

"And?" I probed.

Caleb folded his arms in a fashion that screamed it was none of my business. "Can we help you with something, Beth?"

I forced a laugh. "Yes, Caleb, you can. Where's Philippe?"

He flinched. "I thought he was with you."

"He's not."

He looked to Margarete, and she shook her head.

His eyes met mine. "I haven't seen him all night."

"Maybe he's hanging around where his painting is—"

"I sold the painting," Caleb interrupted.

"You did?"

"Yes, to Amon. Why?"

Mental distortion took over. Rubbing my temples, I asked in disbelief, "Amon bought the painting?"

He sighed in frustration. "Why do you keep questioning everything I'm saying? Yes, Amon bought the painting. So what?"

I spun in every direction, searching the room frantically. "Where is he?"

Margarete touched my arm. "He took the painting and left. What's going on, Beth? What's wrong?"

"I have to find Philippe."

I didn't wait for a reply. Weaving between mortals and immortals alike, I skimmed every face. Not one belonged to the man I sought. Philippe had vanished without saying a word. Did he know about the painting? Had he gone after Amon? Was there a struggle? Were either of them hurt? Was he...? Amon was a god after all...I couldn't even think it. Was I assuming too much because of their earlier exchange? Was I overanalyzing? Where would he go? Home! He'd go home.

I dashed out the front entrance and combed the street for Jon Paul and the car; nothing, not a trace. With fiendish speed I scampered off, racing the wind all the way home. Once inside the house, I bolted up the staircase. Soft whimpers sounded in my ears, and I paused halfway up the stairs. There they were again, higher in pitch and unmistakably female. As I stepped onto the second-floor landing, I peered down the hallway. A glimmer of light flickered from beneath our bedroom door. I crept closer and slowly turned the knob, pushing the door open.

As I edged through the doorway, the image of the naked girl grinding on top of Philippe was forever burned into my brain. My feet rooted into the floor and I bit down on my lip, smothering a gasp. I openly stared. It was like a scene from a violent horror movie you don't want to look at, but at the same time, can't take your eyes off of.

Philippe angled his head toward me. A malicious blaze lit up his eyes as he hurled words inside my head. *Two can play at this game, bitch!* Lifting a finger, he pointed at me and said aloud, "This is my... wife."

She gave me a fleeting glance. Nothing was going to spoil her orgasm, not even his wife. Philippe grabbed her hips and thrust himself into her. That was all she needed, and she screamed in delight. I smashed my hands over my ears and slumped against the wall. Her high-pitched squeals and his feverish grunts grew louder. Shuffling backward, I gripped the doorframe and inched out the door. Hot tears ran down my cheeks. With a brush of my hand I banished them, and my fingers curled into balls of anger. I stormed down the stairs and out the front door. I had one thought and one thought only...*blood!* I craved it. Lots of it.

Blasting off the ground, I barreled headfirst through the dark night, heading straight for Bloodthirst. The red neon lights flickered in the distance, warning me to cut my speed, and I floated downward. With the club's events well underway, the sweet aroma of warm, fresh blood hovered at the cracks behind the closed golden door.

I exposed my fangs and grabbed the latch, itching for a taste.

"Perfect timing, baby vamp."

The arrogant female tone rang in my ears. I knew that voice—the demon! A prickling sensation scurried up my spine. I slowly turned my head in the direction from which the voice had come.

As she extinguished her flames, the intricate engravings and symbols on her armor came to life under the moon's ethereal glow. Her ice-blue eyes twinkled with delight when she said, "You're frightened." She stepped closer. "I haven't come to hurt you. I have news."

I let go of the latch and clutched my hands together so violently they ached. Had she found them? Would justice finally be ours to claim? The scent of blood escaped from inside to encircle my head and ignite my senses. I reached for the handle, hesitated, and stepped toward my foreboding messenger before my most primal instincts forced me to face the door once more.

"Is it blood you want?" She didn't wait for my reply but plucked a man off the street in an instant. At her touch he went limp before she effortlessly propped him up against the wall. "Drink."

He slumped motionless inside her grasp, his mouth hanging open and his eyes glazed over. With my finger, I raised his chin. When I pulled it away his head dropped onto his chest. He didn't flinch, not one muscle. I glared at her. "What did you do to him?"

A satisfied grin animated her charred face. "I stunned him, much as a spider would a fly." She shrugged disinterestedly. "Whether you kill him or not is up to you."

"I don't want to *kill* him. I want his blood."

"Then drink."

Why the goodwill? I searched her eyes, probing deeper into her brain, receiving back only white noise—most likely as she'd intended. She couldn't allow a mere vampire to gain access to the inside of that head of hers. The human's heartbeat stroked my eardrum, distracting me and drawing my gaze back to him. The bulging vein at the side of his neck pulsated. My hands trembled with loss of self-control. I pounced, stabbing his jugular and pulling him into my embrace. The world slipped away. Philippe and the girl no longer mattered; the demon's news, even, became meaningless. There was only me and my blood frenzy. The number ten came and went inside my head...twenty... forty.... Somewhere around one hundred, I retracted my fangs, but I didn't let go. I clung to him, breathing in his intoxicating scent.

Reality finally barged into the moment. Street noise flooded back. People paraded up and down the sidewalk, jabbering about nothing. The demon leaned against the wall, her arms loosely crossed and a wicked gleam dancing in her eyes.

"Welcome back." She winked at me. "Was that good for you?"

I backed away from him, wiping blood from my mouth. I looked to her, concern tainting my voice. "He's still not moving."

She smirked and snapped her fingers.

As if she was a puppeteer pulling his strings, he popped off the wall and stood upright. Maneuvering his way between us, he smiled at me, saying, "Excuse me," as he passed by. I kept my eyes on him as he strolled up the street, continuing on his merry way.

"He appeased your anger, as well as your appetite. You're calmer now," she said, studying me.

Did the demon have similar gifts as I? "How did you know that? Were you inside my head?"

"Mind games are your thing, baby vamp. I feed off emotion." She pointed her grayish-black finger at me. "You were radiating hate."

An image of Philippe and his conquest assaulted the space behind my eyes. I swallowed hard and rubbed at my temple. "Men," I murmured, half-aloud.

She tilted her head at me, confusion written into her expression. "I don't understand your species. Love is a waste of time."

I knew nothing of her world. Was she even capable of love? Did only malice rule her life? I took a step toward her and held out my hand. "My name is Beth. Do you have a name?"

"Why, yes, I do." She stepped closer and extended her hand. "It is Jaffa."

Cool to the touch, her snake-like flesh glided into my palm. I squeezed her hand. "It's nice to formally meet you, Jaffa."

A genuine smile spread across her face. "And you, Beth."

"Sorry about the interruption. You said you have news?"

She released my hand, and a grim expression returned to her face. "I found them in London."

Her words inspired ice to run through my veins. "Osiris, Isis, and Hathor—you found them?"

With an arrogant air, she said, "I did."

"London!" I was incredulous.

"In the Highgate Cemetery."

"We have to tell Amon. Will you come with me to find him?"

She answered without hesitation. "I will."

"How exactly do you travel? Should we walk, fly, take a cab, what?"

She cackled out electric laughter. "I like you, baby vamp." She raised a single ghost-white brow. "I transport my body."

"Well, that's a handy trick. So then, should we meet at Ptah's? The address is—"

She cut me off. "I don't need an address. I need an image."

"An image? I don't have an image."

She tapped a smooth finger against my forehead. "An image in your head is all I need. Think of it."

I conjured up the familiarity of Ptah's ocean estate.

She spread her fingers and pressed them into my scalp for a brief instant. "See you there," she whispered in my ear, and then she was gone.

In the dark sky, I gracefully maneuvered toward Ptah's while the moon watched over me.

She stood on the porch, leaning against the closed door. "Not bad."

I blew on my knuckles, faux polishing them on my shirt afterward. "Thank you." I rapped on the door before noticing the hesitation written into her body language.

Moving farther back, she stood at the porch's edge.

I waved her over. "It's okay."

Her forehead wrinkled with worry. "The owner, where is he? The invitation must be his."

"Ptah and I are like family. He won't mind."

She held her ground. "I'll wait here."

"Nonsense. Come inside."

The door opened and a hand slipped through the frame and pulled me forward by my dress's waist. "I've been waiting for you." Amon's soft lips pressed to the tip of my nose, inciting a giggle from me. He noticed our guest. "I see you've brought a guest?"

"She has a name," I chided. "Jaffa."

He stood tall, asserting his authority in a very unnecessary fashion. "Jaffa, is it?"

"Yes," she said, unimpressed.

Amon relaxed visibly and stepped aside. "Well, don't just stand there. Come inside."

She hesitated, studying him.

I approached her, trying to ease her anxiety. "It's okay. You're welcome. Please, come inside."

The wind stirred, rustling up leaves and tossing them about the porch. Ptah's dry laughter blended with their rustle as he joined us on the front steps. "I don't believe it, a demon on my front porch." The realization of what this meant struck him. "Tell me you have news."

She grinned self-assuredly. "I do."

"Come on in and let's hear it."

Now invited in by the man himself, she adopted a confident swagger and entered Ptah's home.

"Just don't set anything on fire," Ptah stated with an arch of his brow.

Jaffa scowled and, like a match to gasoline, ignited her saffron flames. Brilliant orange made a wide frame around her gray-toned flesh.

"She means no harm," I shouted, rolling my hands into fists. *Please mean none*, I pleaded inside my head.

She exploded with wicked laughter, snuffing the flames out one by one. Smirking, she blew Ptah a kiss. "Kidding."

Spots of color flushed Ptah's cheeks. "That wasn't funny." He glanced over at me and Amon. "Was that funny?" His gaze darted back to her. "Not funny."

She chuckled. "I disagree."

His voice had a tense edge to it. "Did you come here to unnerve me or do you actually have news?"

I came to stand at her side. "She does. She found the three we seek."

Ptah opened his mouth, but no words came out.

Amon edged closer, his gaze intense. "Are you certain?"

She locked eyes with Amon. "They're in London. Hiding in the catacombs underneath Highgate Cemetery."

Ptah looked puzzled. "Not what I expected to hear."

Amon's eyes had become alive with their own fire. "Osiris, Isis, and Hathor—you set eyes on them?"

"Of course, I did," she snapped. "I'm not here to play games."

"When did you last see them?" I asked.

"Earlier this evening. Straight away, I transported back to Castle Beach and ran into you at Bloodthirst."

Amon shot me a wounded look. "You were at Bloodthirst? I thought you went home."

Home...the word meant nothing anymore. My answer came out flat and lifeless. "I'll explain later. First, London." I stood waiting, certain he'd rummage through my thoughts and take what he wanted. He didn't intrude.

In a quiet voice, Jaffa added, "Hunters are tracking them."

"Hunters?" I was surprised. What hunters would have the nerve to track gods?

Ptah spoke to me in a tone meant to reassure. "Hunters have polluted London since the dawn of time. They're nothing but cockroaches."

"Don't be a fool," the demon barked at him. "*Never* underestimate the hunter."

Ptah scoffed, "Fool...ha. I'll have you know—"

Amon cut him short. "Tell me about these hunters."

Her ice-blue eyes sharpened. "They're whisper quiet, and unbelievably cunning. They don't use stakes or guns." She paused dramatically. "They use arrows of fire to kill."

I glanced with uncertainty at Ptah and Amon.

Ptah's eyes widened ever so slightly. "Fire?"

She nodded.

Amon furrowed his brow. "Hunters before have never designed a weapon so clever." He glanced at Ptah. "Members of The Ten threatened by hunters. I won't stand for it. This changes everything. Contact the others. We must all go to London at once."

"I'm going with you," I said firmly.

Amon shook his head. "It's too dangerous. Wait for me here."

I firmed up my resolve and shook my head. "Like hell I will. I played the waiting game once. Not doing it again. There's no way I'm staying behind. I'm going, period."

For several minutes he said nothing as he contemplated my words. "Very well," he agreed as if he had a choice, "but you never leave my side."

I kissed his cheek. "Agreed."

"It's too late tonight to journey to London," Ptah pointed out. "We'll have to sleep away the day and set out at dusk." He turned to the demon. "Hmm, what to do with you?"

Her posture grew rigid, and the tendons in her neck stood out.

I spoke up for her. "She'll stay here with us."

"Can I trust you, demon?" Ptah asked.

"She has a name," I reminded him. "It's Jaffa."

"Very well," Ptah sighed, eyeing me with disdain. "Jaffa, can I trust you?"

She looked him dead in the eye and answered matter-of-factly, "No."

"Well then, you can't stay here," he huffed.

"Nonsense," I said, grabbing her arm and pulling her close to me. "She stays."

Amon folded his arms stubbornly. "Beth, she just admitted we can't trust her."

"We don't have to trust her. I think we just have to believe she will take us to Osiris, Isis, and Hathor. Finding them is all that matters."

Amon smiled at me radiantly. "When did you become such a self-assured vampire?"

"The five years we were apart."

He flashed immediately to my side. "I'm sorry," he whispered in my ear.

I hugged him, pulling him in close. "I don't blame you."

In a flat tone, Jaffa said, "Ah, that's sweet...but am I staying?"

I glanced at Ptah questioningly.

He gave a quick nod. "Fine, but one fire alarm goes off and you're out."

"She's not going to set anything on fire," I assured him, even though I had absolutely no clue what she'd do or not do.

Ptah waved her forward. "Come. I'll show you to one of the rooms."

"I don't sleep."

I took her hands, dragging her away from the front room. "I'll stay with her. We can hang out in the living room and watch the waves."

She shook her head and shooed me toward Amon. "Don't use me as an excuse to avoid telling him what happened."

Amon's curiosity was piqued. "Tell me what?"

"There's nothing to tell."

Jaffa rolled her eyes. "Liar."

Amon nudged me forward. "Come upstairs. We can speak privately in my room."

I gave him a noncommittal nod. Philippe, the girl, the sex—it all left a horrid taste in my mouth. The last thing I wanted to do was rehash it.

Amon hurried me up the stairs and into a bedroom three doors down. Sleek white-gloss furniture, rich black fabrics, and abstract art adorned the spacious room, each piece keeping true to Ptah's modern theme.

To the left, my portrait stood against the wall. Seeing it there was like a punch to the gut. I stumbled, barely managing to catch my fall. The image on the canvas stared back, taunting me. Remembrances of the night flooded my mind: the girl's naked body, Philippe's hands on her hips, the graphic sex right before my eyes. A growl crawled out of my throat. I snatched a book from the shelf and hurled it at the painting. "Bastard!"

Amon rushed to my side, cupping my face in his hands and forcing me to look at him. His eyes searched mine. "Beth, what happened?" He didn't wait for a reply as he entered my head and flipped through my thoughts, witnessing a frame-by-frame blow of Philippe's betrayal. He stepped back, speechless.

I turned away from him. "His actions hurt me, angered me. I didn't even know myself how to process what I saw. How could I tell you?" I looked into his eyes. "But what I do know is you're the one I love, believe that."

Not a hair ruffled, he chuckled. "When have you ever known me to be insecure? You're wounded and angry, and rightfully so. That doesn't mean you don't love me."

In a scathing tone, I said, "I hate him right now."

He stroked my hair, soothing the tension in my body. "Time will take the sting away. I promise. Come to bed. I will hold you until you fall asleep."

I grabbed a handful of my dress. "I've got nothing to change into, just this dress that *he* bought."

"I've got a surprise for you." He ambled over to the closet. "The seller accepted my offer. The penthouse is ours."

I clapped my hands. "Wonderful!" I paused. "But how does that help my wardrobe situation?"

"It doesn't." Throwing the closet doors wide, he added, "But this does."

Oversized sweaters, graphic tees, skinny jeans, and boots—all my favorite articles of clothing—lined the shelves, draped from hangers, and sat in rows along the floor. My gaze darted back and forth, uncertain where to settle first. "Oh my God. When did you do all this?" I ran into his arms and smothered him with kisses. "Thank you!"

He appeared quite pleased with himself. "Oh, here and there. You're happy ? I did well?"

I slipped a sweater off its hanger and hugged it against my chest. "Hell, yes. I knew there was a reason I loved you."

"You mean besides my good looks and charm?"

I gave him a playful shove. "Yes, besides those."

He tucked my hair behind my ears and kissed me. Winking at me, he pulled a drawer open. "I didn't forget about the sexy underwear."

Leaning over his shoulder, I took a peek. He got that right too—all black. I stretched my arms overhead. "I'm so ready to get out of this dress." I peered at the shelves down the length of the closet. "Did you happen to get pajamas?"

Tapping the bottom drawer of the dresser closest to us, he said, "I did."

I rooted through and found a pair of boxer shorts and matching tank. I sighed, "I need sleep."

"I'll let you change." He kissed me again. "See you in bed."

"Our first sleepover," I said, feeling my pulse race.

"Indeed." He slipped out of the closet, partially closing the door behind him.

I stripped off my dress and underwear, tossing them into the hamper in the corner. I changed into the items I'd chosen in a frenzy and then rushed into the bedroom. Amon sat on the bed in dark-blue pajama bottoms, his arms folded across his bare Herculean torso. His emerald-green eyes lit up as they wandered over me.

I couldn't contain my joy as I padded across the wooden floor. I climbed up next to him on the bed, breathless with my heart thumping inside my chest.

He brushed the back of his hand down my cheek. "You're upset. The first time we make love, I don't want Philippe inside your head— only me."

I sighed, my shoulders drooping in defeat. He was right. At the moment, bitterness clouded my heart. Our first time should be special and just between the two of us. Lying with my head on his chest, I conceded, "Then we wait."

He pulled me close, wrapping his strong arms around me and smoothing my hair. Every so often, he kissed my cheek and my forehead. "Good night, my darling Beth."

I softly kissed his lips before curling into his side. "Good night, my love."

****

The intoxicating bouquet of blood plucked me from my dreams. After blinking several times, I finally forced my eyes open and stretched out my hand, reaching for Amon. Instead, my fingers brushed over bedding. I sat straight up, my gaze encompassing the entire room. It was empty, and I was alone. Glancing down at the bed, I discovered a single piece of white stationery trimmed with gold on the pillow beside me. It read, *The others have arrived. Join us downstairs when you wake. Blood is waiting for you, Amon.*

Tossing back the comforter, I climbed out of bed, staggering into the shower and blasting my body with cold water to jolt myself awake. It didn't take long for me to switch gears and crank the hot water knob all the way to the right. A delicious stream of heat rained over my body. I lingered underneath, soaking in the warmth. After toweling off, I combed out my hair and tied it into a loose bun before revisiting my new closet and snatching a white T-shirt emblazoned with the image of a blood-red rose, black skinny jeans, boots, and a black leather jacket. As I looked into the mirror, I nodded at my reflection and went in search of Amon.

At the top of the staircase, I caught the salty, sweet scent of blood rushing up from below. I bolted downstairs, pursuing the scent like a crazed animal. It led me across the foyer, down the hall, and into the formal dining room. Bodies were gathered but I saw no faces, heard no voices; there were only blurred objects in my way. My driving force... blood.

Spread across the burnished tortoiseshell table stood countless tall-stemmed glasses, filled to the rim with a mouthwatering crimson red. Steam floated around the tops and sweat trickled down the side of each glass. I curled my trembling fingers around the stem of a glass, raising it to my lips and drinking deeply. After I'd drained it, I tapped at the bottom of the glass, sucking down the last drop. I quickly grabbed up another, chugging half the glass in one gulp. I felt a trickle escape the corner of my mouth, but I efficiently retrieved the stray drop with my tongue.

As I emptied my second glass, the bloodlust vanished, and my surroundings grew crystal clear. I could see that the whole gang was there, scattered about in cliques as if we were still in high school; the rich and popular represented by The Ten; the outcasts, Margarete and Jaffa; the bad boy, Caleb; and rounded off by the cheating husband, Philippe.

Pacing, fidgeting, and deafening silence plagued the room. Nephthys huddled in Horus's strong embrace, a dull glaze clouding her beautiful gray eyes. Anubis straightened his scarlet tie again and again. Sobek and Khum stood on either side of Horus and Nephthys, unnaturally still, like book ends. Ptah overplayed his role as host, constantly refilling glasses with blood. Amon rested his hand on Horus's shoulder, uncharacteristically still and silent. Caleb, Margarete, and Jaffa hung in the background, staring blankly amongst themselves. Philippe lurked in the corner, arms pinned fast against his stomach, darting nervous glances at me.

Amon bent to whisper something in Horus's ear, then left his side to approach me. "Good evening, my darling. Sleep well?"

I stroked his arm. "Like a dream." I gave a nod toward the cluster of The Ten. "Lots of tension in that corner of the room?"

He glanced over his shoulder at them. "Horus and Nephthys can't reach Osiris and Isis. They fear the worst."

"The worst...you mean hunters? How could human hunters capture three vampire gods? It doesn't make any sense to me."

Amon pointed in Jaffa's direction. "According to her, it's entirely possible."

Jaffa twisted her head in our direction. She made her way over to us, grinning as she approached. "Are you two talking about me?"

Amon sneered at her and opened his mouth to speak, but I cut him off. "These hunters you speak of, are they truly capable of ensnaring three vampire gods?"

She leveled her gaze at me, heavy with solemnity. "Yes, their arrogance will be their downfall. They consider themselves to be quite invincible. That is their weakness. That will be their undoing."

Amon lifted a single brow. "I think you underestimate their power."

She forced out a laugh. "I think it's impossible for you to be objective."

"I most certainly can. I am aware danger is present in this world, even to a being as powerful as myself."

She appraised him up and down. "We'll see."

"Gods, vampires, demons, and hunters—we're all vulnerable. Watching each other's backs will be what keeps us alive," I reasoned.

Jaffa nodded. "Couldn't have said it better myself."

Amon placed his hands on my shoulders. "You don't have to go. It's safer here."

I was abundantly clear the first time he'd brought it up. It was pointless to state it again. "I'm going. End of story."

His eyes were filled with concession. "Okay, Beth. Point taken."

Someone tapped my right shoulder. Turning, I found myself staring into Philippe's gray-blue eyes. Shame weighed heavily in his expression. His eyes focused on the floor. "May I speak with you?"

"No," I snapped, turning my back on him.

"Please," he begged, his voice strained.

I faced him, folding my arms like a shield over my chest. I mustered up my most stony, silent gaze and laid it on him.

"I need to explain. Can we go somewhere private?"

I blinked disbelievingly, shaking my head. "I don't need an explanation. What I walked in on was explanation enough." He reached for my hand, and I jerked it away. Raising my voice, I pointed to the farthest end of the room. "Go."

He clasped his hands in front of his chest and shook them in desperation. "Beth, please, I need—"

I turned, full of fury, toward Jaffa. "Can you just set his ass on fire?"

A glimmer of eager light flashed in her eyes. "Really?"

Philippe shuffled back a couple of steps.

Caleb sprinted across the room, stepping between Philippe and the demon. "No, you cannot." He threw a nasty scowl in my direction. "What's wrong with you?"

I jabbed a finger at Philippe. "Ask him."

Caleb grabbed Philippe by the arm and dragged him off to the far corner of the room...and out of harm's way. Amon appeared at my side to escort me outside into the backyard and sat with me on one of the lounge chairs. He opened his mouth, no doubt to criticize me, but then stopped short. His hand came to rest on my knee. "You can't have this mess with Philippe clouding your judgment in London. You'll need to keep your wits about you."

I rested my head on his shoulder. "You're right, but I can't allow him to apologize. I want him to suffer." Throwing my head back, I groaned, "I'm acting like a child."

He kissed the tip of my nose. "Yes, you are."

"Hey, you're not supposed to agree with me. You're supposed to tell me I have every right to feel betrayed."

He took my hands and stood, pulling me into his embrace. He held me close, running a hand over my back. "You have every right to feel betrayed."

I kissed his left cheek, then his right, and then his lips, lingering there. "Thank you," I whispered.

CHAPTER 8

Exercising our vampire wings, our group of eleven, bearing tote bags and backpacks, landed inside the foggy streets of London, dangerously close to dawn and the destructive rays of the sun. Ptah squinted, his gazed traveling up the street. Setting down the cooler packed with blood, he glanced over his shoulder at me. "Where's Jaffa? She should have arrived before us."

"Here," she called out, drifting like an apocalyptic angel from the fog.

Ptah warily eyed the brightening sky. "We need shelter and fast. Got any ideas, Jaffa?"

Her eyes shifted around inside her skull, as if she were contemplating leaving us out to broil. The corner of her mouth twitched into an a slight smile. Her blank expression returned just as quickly, and she rattled off, "Park House is the closest, on Anson Road, but their rooms are few. They have maybe twelve at most."

Ptah shot her a look full of gratitude. "We'll take our chances. Listen up. Head to Park House, Anson Road."

Amon lingered in the street. "I'd forgotten the depth of London's charm. It leaves me breathless every time." He brushed his lips across my cheek. "But nothing can compare to the flutter in my heart when I gaze into your sea-green eyes. If there should ever come a time when we must part, let it be the last day of my immortal life."

Euphoria swelled inside my heart and a shudder of pleasure rippled through me. "I love you," I whispered.

Under the dim streetlights of Highgate, our lips touched in a tender, yet passionate, kiss.

Anubis thrust a rigid arm between us, prying us apart. "Now's not the time, lovebirds." He pointed at the sky. "Sun's rising."

Stripping off his backpack, Amon shed his coat and threw it over my head. "Hold on," he commanded, tucking me under his arm.

We blasted off the ground in desperate pursuit of our companions. Jaffa's ghost-white dreadlocks stood out like a beacon of light on the streets below us. "There," I shouted, extending a finger in her direction.

He aimed our bodies at her, landing inches from where she waited in front of a red-brick Victorian mansion with white trim. At the entrance, Jaffa waved all of us up the walkway like a tour guide. Footsteps pounded against the sidewalk, rushing up from behind.

Anubis appeared between Amon and me, clapping Amon on the back. "I love it when you barrel away like a bat out of hell."

Amon beamed. "It is quite impressive, isn't it?"

"Very." Anubis gave him a thumbs up.

Jaffa waved at us, urging us forward. "What's wrong with you?" She pointed to the sky and then to the three of us. "Sun plus vampire equals poof. Get your asses inside."

Amon ushered me and Anubis through the open doors. Jaffa didn't follow. She turned back toward the street, and I ran after her.

Amon put his arm out to stop me. "Beth, there isn't time."

I tried to remove the obstacle, but he wouldn't budge. "Jaffa," I cried.

She faced me and shook her head. "I can't go in there, Beth. I'll terrify them. I won't get through the front door."

"Yes, you will. Come here. Let me help."

She approached hesitantly and shrugged. "I don't see how you can help."

"We'll see." I shook off Amon's coat and held it up. "Here, slip this on."

Shaking her head, she put on the coat. "Happy now?"

Folding the lapel upward, I hid her neck and part of her jaw line. I rearranged her dreadlocks, pulling them forward to cover most of her face. I shoved her hands inside the pockets, then stood back to look her over. "Perfect."

She glanced at her reflection in the window, her eyes growing large. "Not bad, baby vamp."

Amon gently tossed the two of us over the threshold. "Get inside already," he said, closing the door on a glistening ray of sunlight inching up the porch. But inside, every wall held a large window, beckoning the morning light to shine in.

All twelve of us crowded the front desk, dodging the beams of daylight streaming in through the windows. Jaffa stayed close to me, keeping her head down and her eyes on the floor.

A fair-haired young man behind the counter plastered a polite smile on his face. "May I help you?"

Ptah placed his hands on the counter. "Yes, do you have any rooms available?" He looked over his shoulder and then back at the young man. "Twelve to be exact."

"The hotel is half full. We have six rooms available."

"We'll double up," Ptah quickly replied.

"How long will you be staying?"

Horus stepped forward, an air of readiness about him. "We can't be certain how long it will take."

Nephthys twisted the ornate bracelet encircling her arm. "We aren't leaving without them."

The young man furrowed his brow. "Excuse me?"

Anubis approached the front desk, straightening his tie and adjusting his jacket. "We're meeting some friends, and our plans are up in the air right now." He dug into his pocket and produced a credit card, shot a look of warning at Horus and Nephthys, and then turned his attention toward the young man. "We'll pay up front for one week."

The young man nodded and ran the card through a machine tucked under the counter. He placed the receipt on the counter, handing Anubis his card and a pen.

Anubis's hand flew across the tiny sheet of paper. "Now, the rooms, please," he said, slapping the pen and signed receipt onto the counter.

Sobek eyed the windows, buttoning up his jacket. "It is imperative they be very dark."

"Sir?"

Shifting to the right to avoid a glistening patch of sunlight, Khum clarified, "Sunlight cannot disturb us."

The young man bobbed his head up and down. "All our rooms have window coverings, sir."

A golden stream of heat bled through the nearest window, creeping over me and stinging my flesh like a thousand bees. Flinching, I gripped Amon's arm. "The sun," I whispered frantically.

Amon stepped behind me, shielding my body with his own. In a sharp tone, he queried, "We are all quite exhausted from our flight. We just want to crash. Can't you hurry this up?"

The clerk whirled around, grabbing the remaining keys off the wall in a panic, and dropped them on the counter. Scooping up a clipboard, he thrust it at Anubis. "I need you to sign."

"Of course." Anubis reached out and scribbled his signature.

"Your rooms are up the stairwell and to the right. We serve breakfast every morning in the kitchen, and behind us there is a cozy sitting room with lots of natural light for reading."

I snickered internally. *You missed the mark on both. How about a steaming mug of blood or a study lit by moonlight?*

He flipped over one of the keys. "Room number's on the back. Do you need help with your bags?"

"Thank you, we've got it covered," Anubis said in a rush, gathering up the handful of keys.

We scattered, scampering up the stairs and into the dark hallway of the second floor. Halfway down the long, narrow corridor, Anubis stopped and held up the keys. "There are six rooms; pair up."

With some shifting about, pairs began to emerge; Amon and I, Horus and Nephthys, Sobek and Khum, Ptah and Anubis, Caleb and Margarete...leaving Philippe and Jaffa. Definitely not a favorable paring.

Caleb softly kissed Margarete's cheek. "Those two cannot share a room. Would you be a dear and pair up with Jaffa? I can room with Philippe."

She forced a smile. "You owe me." She turned her back on him reluctantly, joining Jaffa.

Caleb moved to stand next to Philippe. "Done. Now pass out the damn keys."

Anubis took his time handing out the keys, saving Caleb and Philippe for last. He smirked, waiting nearly a full minute before dropping the key into Caleb's palm.

"I think the centuries are starting to get to you, old man," Caleb retorted as he closed his fist around his key.

Anubis only chuckled before trotting back to Ptah.

Men, human or vampire, always trying to outdo one another. I just wanted to flop down on my bed and sleep.

Ptah popped the lid off the cooler, passing out a bag of blood to each person. "Should be room temperature by dusk." Raising a finger, he warned, "Drink sparingly. We have enough for two days at the most. Once we are forced to feed in public, we will draw attention to ourselves and alert the hunters."

Sobek bared his fangs. "I will snap the neck of any hunter foolish enough to cross my path."

Khum joined in on the pissing match. "And I will butcher any who might slip by you."

Jaffa shook her head at them. "You all reek of overconfidence. It will lead to your demise."

Anubis laughed arrogantly. "Nonsense. We are gods, love."

Ptah put his hand on her shoulder. "We will heed your advice." He shot a look of warning at Anubis. Turning to the rest of us, he said, "We've got a long night ahead of us. Go; get some rest."

With keys and blood bags in hand we split off, seeking out our rooms. Amon and I scanned the numbers on the doorways until we finally arrived at our room, nestled at the far end of the hallway. The bed on the other side of that door was calling my name. My eyelids grew heavy and a yawn escaped me. Dropping my tote on the floor, I leaned heavily against Amon.

I dragged my tote bag into the room as Amon unlocked the door. A smothering beam of heat struck my face, and I stumbled backward until I became plastered against the wall. Morning's golden fingers stretched the length of the room, lighting it on fire. Droplets of sweat trickled down my brow. My skin puckered, sizzled, and blistered. I cried out, ducking toward the floor, and threw the tote in front me, blocking the sun.

Amon tossed the bags of blood and his backpack aside, dashed for the window, and yanked the cord, drawing the curtains into a solid, impenetrable line. Velvety darkness settled over the room. The sun's blinding light caught me off guard, leaving me paralyzed with fear, reminding me of its immense power over our existence.

"Are you all right?" Amon asked.

"I...I think so." With his help, I staggered over to the king-sized bed and collapsed onto the mattress.

Amon closed the door and laid the bags of blood out on top of the dresser before climbing onto the bed with me. "That was unpleasant."

"To say the least." I buried my head into the pile of pillows. "I'm too exhausted to undress," I managed to say.

Amon kicked off his shoes but nothing more. "I second that."

****

After the day's much-needed rest, a hot shower, and a change of clothes, Amon and I gathered with the others at Swain's Lane, just outside Highgate Cemetery. The unkempt graveyard, enclosed by an enormous wrought iron gate, enshrouded the entire west end of the street. Peaks of sparse, leafless trees and crumbling monuments stretched beyond the railing, perhaps in an attempt to escape the melancholy of the forsaken graveyard.

Ptah scowled and, keeping his voice low, whispered, "As Jaffa pointed out, we can't be too careful. Keep your eyes and ears vigilant."

Horus pursed his lips cynically. "We're wasting time standing here. This 'take heed' speech is inconsequential."

Khum joined Horus and stated in a manner meant to fortify his friend's position, "Agreed."

Sobek spoke up as well. "Horus is right. We are The Ten. We are gods."

Nephthys came to join the more cavalier group of vampires and rested her hand on her hip. "Mankind fears us, not the other way around." She sneered at Jaffa. "You are obviously not well-versed in your knowledge of vampire gods."

Jaffa haughtily retorted, "We shall see."

Caleb slapped Jaffa on the back. "You tell her, Smokey."

Jaffa's ice-blue eyes darkened like a thunderstorm brewing.

Margarete lightly touched Jaffa's shoulder. "Ignore him."

"Come, everyone, listen up." Ptah made an attempt to reestablish the proper level of gravity to the moment.

Philippe leaned casually against one of the streetlights, arms crossed, eyes fixed on the ground in an untroubled manner.

Anubis straightened his jacket, ensuring the perfect amount of his white linen shirt peeked out from his lapel.

No one seemed to pay attention to Ptah's efforts. I stood in the middle of the lot of proud peacocks, strutting about and preening their colorful feathers. Jaffa was right; overconfidence might very well become their downfall this night.

Amon pressed his lips to my ear. "My eyes and ears are open, even if theirs aren't."

I glanced toward the cemetery gates. A solitary stream of moonlight danced across the coiled chain, securing the entrance. Glancing back at him, I said, "That won't be enough."

As we drew nearer, I caught a wider glimpse of the cemetery. Shadows ducked in and out of the trees and among the gravestones, toying with my imagination...one in particular. Its dense form crouched beneath the drooping branches of a large tree. I peered closer, and whatever it was shrank backward, vanishing into the brush. "Did you see that?" I darted to the gate, gripped the wrought iron, and scrutinized the area with my enhanced vision.

Amon rushed over to join me. "See what?"

"A form...like a person." My eyes traveled back to the area, finding no trace of the dark mass that had been there a moment before.

Horus barged between us, fearlessly snapping the chain and prying the gates apart. "I'm going in."

Nephthys, Sobek, Khum, and Anubis charged after him like seasoned warriors.

Caleb stepped through the opening, glanced back at me, and grinned, teasing. "It's a cemetery, Red; notorious for being creepy, right?" He waved me forward. "Come on, you'd think you were still human."

I held my ground. Graveyard or not, I'd seen someone or something out there.

"I believe you," Philippe quietly said as he passed by, heading after Caleb.

I watched him walk away, a little surprised. Were his words merely a ploy to smooth things over or did he truly believe me?

Margarete nudged my shoulder. She yanked up her sleeve to reveal the tiny clusters of goose bumps scurrying over her flesh. "I can feel them."

I met her eyes. "Feel whom?"

She shuddered as she ran her hands over her skin. "Lost souls. The graveyard is crawling with them." Ducking inside the gate, she moved close to Caleb and added, "Probably what you saw."

Had I actually caught sight of my first ghost? I lingered at the entrance, a touch unnerved.

Jaffa approached, her gaze combing the cemetery. "She's right; spirits are present; but...."

"But what?" I probed.

She eyed me in a deliberate sort of way. "But you don't see them, you *feel* them."

I shrugged. "I didn't feel anything."

"Exactly," she clarified. "You saw."

"Doesn't matter," Amon said, snuggling me into his ribcage. "Keep your guard up and stay close to me."

Wiggling to try to gain an inch of personal space, I mildly protested. "Like I have a choice."

He raised his brows at me. "You don't."

I let out an overinflated groan.

Ptah shook his head. "She's a big girl, Amon. She can take care of herself."

"Thank you, Ptah."

Amon loosened his grip just a hair, shooing Ptah away. "Move along, troublemaker."

Ptah merely chuckled before turning his attention to Jaffa. He waved her forward. "Go," he ordered, like an army lieutenant. "I'll head up the rear."

Jaffa shook her head stubbornly and pushed him over the threshold and into the graveyard. "Bad idea. I'll head up the rear."

As we walked across the sacred ground with Jaffa following behind, dried brushwood crackled beneath our footsteps. Granite, ivory, and marble tombstones stood, scattered about, some completely covered over by the vast array of undergrowth. Angels, crosses, lions, dogs, and even a piano stood carved in permanence to honor the departed lying beneath them. Ancient stone crypts towered above us, framing the dirt pathways. My eyes took in the crumbling doorways. In a haunting, romantic way it touched my immortal heart. They'd made me forget why we were there.

Up ahead, Nephthys let out a gasp, shuffling back a few steps.

Horus bared his fangs and actually growled.

Sobek and Khum stood rigidly, their fists clenched.

I heard Caleb blurt out, "Good God."

Margarete turned away and grabbed onto Caleb's arm.

Philippe skidded to a stop and stood completely still.

Anubis pushed his way through the entire group. He peered down, then covered his mouth.

Ptah broke into a run, coming to a grinding halt once he reached the others. "Bloody hell," he exclaimed.

I shot Amon a worried look. "What's going on?"

"I have no idea," he said, his gaze fixed on the others.

Jaffa, Amon, and I scurried up the path, pushing our way through. Two charred bodies lay harpooned together by a flaming arrow, obstructing the path. In shock, I took in the sight of their charcoal-like, shriveled, still-smoldering vampire flesh. My core was seized by a sudden cold, a bone-chilling sensation that penetrated every fiber of my being. I clutched at Amon's arm, clamping a hand over my mouth. Even in death, they clung to one another, their faces frozen in a horrified scream. Specks of white ash danced in the moonlight, littering the ground around them.

"Who did this to them?" I whispered.

"Hunters killed them," a male voice called out from deep within the shadows.

Amon pushed me behind him. "Who's there? Show yourself," he demanded.

A tall, gaunt figure stepped out and into the moonlight. Streaks of gray peppered his short dark hair, and sunken craters stole the form from his frail, pale face. He was a vampire, yes, but one starving for blood. What had caused him to deprive himself of human blood sustenance?

He crept along the path toward us like an old man. Extending his bony hand, he introduced himself. "My name is Ian."

Amon shook his hand with a firm grip that looked to me to be too much for the bony vampire. "I am Amon." He pulled me forward. "And this is Beth."

"I'm honored to meet you, Amon." He turned to me and smiled in a shy sort of way with his thin, dry lips.

I reached out my hand. "Hello, Ian."

Ian enclosed my hand in his own weak grip. Sadness dulled his dark-brown eyes. "You're very beautiful. I wish my appearance wasn't so...ghastly."

"Nonsense," I said, giving his hand a gentle squeeze.

The others edged closer, with hard glares dissecting him as if he were a frog in a biology class. Horus broke free from Nephthys's grasp and approached the blackened corpses so he could pull the smoking arrow from their bodies. They crumbled apart and floated away, two once-powerful immortal beings now reduced to dust. He pulverized what was left of the arrow in his fists, a feral growl building inside his chest.

Ptah explained the situation to Ian. "There are three members of The Ten who have disappeared, and they must be found." He gestured to Nephthys. "One looks very similar to her. Have you seen them?"

Ian nodded at him. "Yes, I've seen them. They stayed with us for a short time."

Horus pushed Ptah out of the way, his gaze darting toward Ian. "Where? Where did they stay?"

Ian pointed beyond them to a cluster of trees. "There, in the catacombs beneath the cemetery."

Caleb curled his upper lip in disgust. "Good God, how foul! Is your clan abnormal in some way? Hideous to the eye, perhaps?"

Margarete jabbed her elbow into Caleb's side. He feigned innocence, widening his eyes and shrugging his shoulders as if he couldn't imagine how he might have offended anyone.

Ian shook his head in answer to Caleb's outburst. "We're afraid. This is why we live in the shadows." He gestured to his emaciated body. "Look at me. We very rarely venture out, even to feed. The hunters hesitate to pursue us underground, which is why we've made it our home."

"How many are you?" Anubis queried.

"There are seven of us left." Ian's tone sounded bleak.

"Left?" I hadn't missed that.

Ian's eyes grew cold. "Hunters got to them. Their burning arrows falling from the sky have killed many. Others have simply vanished. These hunters appear and vanish like ghosts in the night."

Jaffa pushed her way through to Ptah. "Something feels off," she whispered anxiously. "Be on your guard."

He looked at her questioningly. "How so?"

Suddenly, she cocked her head. "Silence," she snapped.

Amon barely had time to cry out, "Beth—"

A blur of orange ripped away my flesh as whizzing, slashing sounds drowned out his voice. The smell of burnt flesh filled the air as I clutched my bloody cheek against my trembling palm. I struggled to comprehend the confusion surrounding me as I was knocked to the ground by a sharp burst of shooting pain.

Fireworks erupted throughout the graveyard as flaming arrows plummeted to the earth, creating thick clouds of smoke. A raging inferno of deadly fires ravaged the once-peaceful cemetery. I squinted through the haze as eerie shadows flickered across the tombstones engulfed in scorching heat. Hysterical screams filled my ears. As everyone fled, I tried to locate Amon.

"Run! Hide!" Ian shrieked, his voice filled with panic.

Emerald-green eyes glimmered in the distance. "Amon!" I charged forward, dodging the arrows whizzing through the air. Margarete appeared out of nowhere, slamming into me. With a thud, I hit the ground. Scrambling upright, I scanned the sky, turning toward Margarete, who stood rooted in the dirt. Grabbing her arm, I shouted, "Keep moving!"

"No, I can't."

I shook her shoulders, trying to snap her out of her state of paralyzed fear. "You can."

"Noooo," she cried.

Arrows whooshed behind us. I spun to find two of them barreling straight for us.

Yanking at her hand, I screamed, "Run, Margarete!" But I knew we couldn't outrun them.

In the seconds before the arrows struck Margarete and me, Jaffa snatched them out of mid-flight. Observing her surroundings, she narrowed her eyes to focused on a canopy of branches and hurled the arrows back into the tress.

An eerie shadow fell over a figure dangling from a tree branch as a load groan echoed from above.

"They're in the trees," she shouted, leaping into the air.

Horus rocketed after her. Nephthys, Sobek, and Khum half-seconds behind. Ptah and Anubis took flight, spreading their arms and snarling in a pitch that made my skin crawl.

Amon suddenly appeared within my grateful sight, rushing toward us, grabbing each of us by an arm and dragging us to relative safety behind a towering monument carved in the likeness of an angel. Pushing me to the ground, he barked out, "Stay low."

Margarete didn't hesitate to drop to her knees, hovering next to me. "We won't move," she promised, gazing up at him with wide, frightened eyes.

I stubbornly protested. "Speak for yourself."

Amon peered more closely at me. "You're hurt." Stabbing a fang into his finger, he smeared his blood across my cheek. "Better?"

Relief washed over me as the burning pain subsided. "Much better," I replied.

Caleb and Philippe emerged from the haze, running toward us. As they crouched behind the monument, they shielded Margarete and I with their bodies.

Moments later, Ian bolted from wherever he had been hiding. His eyes were wide with fear, and his breath came in ragged gasps as he sprinted toward us. Behind him, the sound of arrows whizzing through the air grew closer, urging him to run faster. In a panic, he scrambled behind Caleb and huddled against Margarete.

As Amon looked at Philippe and Caleb, he said, "Watch them closely. Keep them safe."

"We will," Philippe replied gallantly as if he were once again a knight protecting his castle.

Amon's eyes softened. "Thank you," he said, before following the others and vanishing into the trees.

The five of us sat motionless, waiting. I couldn't see a thing between the twist of interlocking branches. A dense wall of leaves blocked my view. Whispers of wind, chirping crickets, and the croak of a lone frog were the only sounds to be heard. The moonlight exposed tiny beads of sweat across Caleb's brow. With a swipe of his hand, he brushed them away. Philippe didn't move a muscle, his breaths spaced and shallow. Margarete hid her face between Caleb's shoulder blades, shivering without cessation. Ian jerked his head in every direction, like a twitchy lizard trying to spot any potential signs of danger.

A bloodcurdling shriek penetrated the near-silence, raising the hairs on my arms. I jumped to my feet, peering into the darkness. "Who screamed? Hunter or vampire?"

Philippe seized my jacket and yanked me back down. "It's not safe," he whispered into my ear.

Margarete mumbled into Caleb's back, "It was a hunter."

Choking, gurgles, and screams rang out...then another, and another, and another. I shrank back. "They're killing them, all of them. I can't...I can't listen to their screams." Clamping my hands over my ears, I attempted to drown out the cries and death rattles, only to witness the horror of severed body parts tumbling from the sky like some kind of macabre, passing rainstorm.

Philippe pulled me close, tucking my face inside his coat. I didn't pull away. I couldn't face the death we'd brought to these mortal creatures. Hunter or not, no one deserved such a gruesome death. How long I huddled in Philippe's arms—seconds, minutes, hours—I couldn't say before the sound of Caleb's voice reached my ears.

"It's over," Caleb replied, exhaling deeply. "They're coming back."

Pulling away from Philippe and rising to my feet, my gaze fell upon the warriors marching across the graveyard, chins held high, shoulders back, and their clothes spattered and dripping with human blood.

Amon stopped in front of me. He must have read something which opposed the way I was feeling in my expression. "We didn't have a choice. It was either us or them."

I simply stared at his blood-covered body, failing to call to mind the right thing to say in response.

Brushing blood from her armor, Jaffa shook her head at me. "Don't you mourn them, baby vamp. Not one of them would think twice about shooting an arrow through your immortal heart."

Caleb applauded the group with great enthusiasm. "Smokey's right, Red; to hell with the hunters." He cocked his head, placed his finger on his chin, and recited, "To die, or not to die, that is the question." He looked me in the eyes to drive the answer home. "I choose not to die."

Margarete ignored Caleb and approached Jaffa. "How many of them were there?"

"Nine."

I clutched at my stomach as I whispered, "Nine poor, foolish souls."

Ian scowled, and there was an edge to his tone when he said, "And nine more will take their place. They're like a hydra's head. Cut one down and another will spring up to take its place."

Ptah had said something very similar when all this had begun. I knew nothing of a hunter's mind. What drove them to kill our kind? Were they alone in the world? Did they need a place to belong or fit in?

A drop of rain hit my nose, interrupting my thoughts, and I lifted my head to look up. In the distance, pebble-gray clouds rumbled, quaked, and opened up. Buckets of rain poured from above, showering the grounds with its watery fit of fury and, thankfully, washing away the blood.

Ian waved us forward. "Come. We can take cover underground."

We slopped through mud puddles, following Ian beneath the earth and into the musty, foul-smelling catacombs of Highgate Cemetery. As we descended deeper into the cave the darkness intensified, creeping up behind us like a demon in the night. The asphyxiating stench of death lingered thick in the air. Slipping off my drenched jacket, I shoved it under my nose to breathe in a little freshness from the rain.

Amon put his arm around me and confided another secret to me. "Use the power of your mind to eliminate the stench. Think of a much-loved fragrance and let it come alive inside your brain. Your surroundings will become infused with that scent."

The image of a gigantic bouquet of roses popped into my head. The orange-sized buds bloomed, spreading open and releasing their delicious perfume, overpowering the decomposing death all around us.

Fresh air rushed into my lungs, and I lowered my jacket. I squeezed Amon's arm. "Thank you."

He kissed the top of my head. "Welcome."

Ian weaved along, leading us down the winding path and guiding us further into the secret mausoleum harboring his undead clan. Lanterns illuminated the final curve into their shelter within the earth's crust. Ian pushed open a heavy steel door and waved us inside.

More lanterns added light to the small, murky cave. I moved to the center of the room and my gaze fell upon seven skeleton-like vampires, slumped around a long rectangular table covered with the carcasses of dead rats. Gray-white flesh stretched over their fragile bodies. Their dull eyes and hair announced how greatly they'd been deprived of blood.

Ian gestured toward them. "This is all that's left of my family."

One by one they slowly rose, hanging onto the edge of the table for balance. Ian neared a young male vampire with curly reddish-blond hair and crystal-blue eyes. "This is Brice. He spent the most time with Osiris."

In two strides Amon stood inches from Brice, peering at him with determination in his eyes. "What did the two of you talk about?"

Brice's lips spread into a half smile. "Joshua."

Anubis smirked. "Kohath's idealistic child; I remember him." He waved a finger at Brice. "Be sure you don't follow in his footsteps."

I looked from Anubis to Brice. "Who is Joshua?"

"He was my maker," Brice said in a voice lined with sorrow.

"Was?" I questioned.

"Joshua was a creature composed of kindness and generosity. His vision of vampires and humans sharing the world as one got him killed."

Anubis clasped Brice's shoulder in a gesture of comfort. "It was a great vision."

Horus came forward, injecting himself into the conversation. "Why Joshua? What did they want to know?"

Brice shrugged. "He didn't say. He wanted to know if I knew where he'd been turned? Had he ever gone back there? If so, how frequent were his visits?"

Amon demanded, "And what did you tell them?"

"He was turned in Edinburgh by Karra. He did go back...at least twice a month."

Horus blurted out, "They're traveling to Edinburgh?"

"Must be," Amon said, his eyes bright and focused. "But to what location in the town?"

A blank expression claimed Brice's face. "That I don't know. But they left in a hurry without any regard for the danger posed by the hunters."

"When?" Horus probed.

"Two days ago," Brice said.

Nephthys clutched at one of the bracelets dangling from her arm, twisting it nervously back and forth. "We must go after them."

Sobek and Khum nodded in agreement, scowls crossing their brows.

Jaffa cleared her throat, drawing everyone's attention. Twirling a dreadlock around her finger, she said, "They haven't left. I still sense their energy."

Ptah suggested, "We should split up and search in both places."

"I'll go to Edinburgh." Caleb offered. "It's my hometown, and I know it well. Philippe, Margarete, are you up for bagpipes and castles?"

Margarete nudged his ribs. "You aren't going anywhere without me."

"I'm in too," Philippe said.

Ptah's gaze traveled over the skinny, listless vampires. He looked over his shoulder at Caleb. "Take Ian and his family to The Council's haven. They need blood, rest, and shelter."

Four of the most animated vampires immediately shed tears of joy.

Ian's eyes glowed as he placed his hand upon his chest. He gestured toward his family. "Thank you for your kindness."

Ptah answered, "No need to thank me. We take care of our own."

Ian told his family. "Grab your belongings. Hurry."

As the group gathered up what little they had, Ptah pulled Jaffa aside. "Go with them. Caleb, Philippe, and Margarete will need your power to protect them against the missing three, should you happen upon them."

Jaffa smirked at him. "I will do this, but hear me now, vampire god; I am not your servant. Not now, not ever."

"Understood," Ptah said, returning a smirk of his own.

We cleared out of the catacombs and into a light drizzle falling from the sky. It was a relief to come back out into the cleanliness of the falling rain. Outside the cemetery gates we parted ways. Ptah, Sobek, Khum, Nephthys, Anubis, Amon, and I watched until the others disappeared from sight. We then headed up the street, dragging our tired bodies back to the hotel for a shower, dry clothes, and most likely a glass of wine...or two.

Inside the lobby, Amon and I peeled off our damp coats while the others went straight upstairs. Amon shook rain from his hair. "I'm in desperate need of a hot shower."

"Well, I need a drink. I'm gonna see if the kitchen has any wine."

He leaned over to kiss me. "Bring me a glass too."

"Of course."

I watched him jog up the stairs before continuing down the hallway, listening to the rainwater slosh in my boots. As I approached the sitting room, I noticed a man seated in a high-back chair. His legs were crossed, a book in his hand, and he was laughing softly as he tucked his carrot-red hair behind his ears. He seemed to blend seamlessly into the surroundings. *Wait a minute. Was that...? No, it couldn't be...could it?*

I shuffled backward to halt in the doorway, gripping the frame and staring at the man. I inched into the room, stopping dead center, waiting for him to turn his head. It seemed an eternity passed before he angled his head in my direction. Greenish-blue eyes and a face full of freckles greeted me with shock.

My hand flew to my chest. "Danny?"

He popped out of the chair, dropping the book on the floor. "Oh my God, Beth! It's you."

Laughing out loud, I ran to him and threw my arms around his neck. "I can't believe it."

His arms came around me, hugging me tightly. Then his arms jerked away from me as his body stiffened. Holding me at arm's length, he peered into my eyes and flinched but didn't let me go. His words came out slowly, as if in a daze. "You're one of them. He turned you."

"It's all right," I assured him. "I won't hurt you. I could never hurt you."

He recovered from the shock as fast as it came on and brought me back into an embrace, pinning me against his body with his arms. "I'm so sorry."

I held him tighter, rubbing his back. "You don't have to be sorry."

"Oh, but I do," he said in a cold, bitter tone.

He wasn't making sense. I pulled back just a hair. "For what?"

"For this."

A prick at the base of my neck set off a panic alarm inside my brain. Danny meant me harm! Heaviness spread limb by limb until I couldn't move and couldn't speak. I slumped forward against my long-lost love... and friend...and watched Danny's lips spread into a sadistic grin as he said, "Got ya." My vision blurred, my lashes fluttered, and darkness came.

CHAPTER 9

I opened my eyes, blinked, and then let them close. A faint *drip, drip, drip* echoed inside my ears. Something hard and cold lay beneath me, making my flesh ache to the bone. Dull pain ricocheted around in my head. Rubbing my fingertips against my temples, I sucked in a deep breath of musty air. Where the hell was I? Danny's face blazed against the surface of my brain. How could Danny be involved in any of this? I bolted upright, forcing my eyes fully open.

Rows of rusty bars, fluorescent lights, a leaky roof, and cracked cement floors materialized once my vision cleared. I centered on the tarnished, bulky padlock restraining the cell door. Was this a prison? I shoved my hands into my bone-dry coat pockets and patted the fabric outside all over. Not a drop of rainwater. It would have taken hours to dry out. I took a mental note: *Been here several hours, possibly more.*

A low, guttural groan sounded from my left. My eyes darted in its direction. A man lay there, curled into the cell bars, whimpering into his mud-streaked hands. Filth and grime encrusted his soiled clothes, and his bare feet were peppered with blisters.

I edged across the floor, my hand stretched before me. Bending down, I gently rolled him over. "Osiris," I gasped, falling back onto my knees. He didn't react. Brushing his shaggy brown hair out of his eyes, I leaned over him again. "Osiris, can you hear me?"

He squinted, locking his gaze on me. He clutched desperately at my arms, whispering, "We have to get out of here."

This was not the mischievous yet poised Osiris I knew. The crazed look written across his sunken face frightened me. "Where are we?"

His eyes darted about. "A dungeon of sorts...for vampires."

I glanced over his shoulder, scanning the row of cells. "How do you mean? What's happened here?"

A vein in the center of his forehead pulsated as he ground out his words from between clenched teeth. "Hunters drained my blood, starved me, shot me up with drugs, and flooded this cell with sunlight.

Something in this place seems to drain our powers." He shook his head, thinking better of his statement. "Maybe it's just the lack of blood."

My mind conjured up the worst possible outcome...death by flaming arrow. Osiris was right. We needed to find a way out. Internally I shouted out to Amon, ***Please come find me!*** Before facing Osiris, I took a second or two to collect myself. Returning my attention to Osiris, I said, "Our circumstances are rather grim."

"You think?"

Clearly Osiris would be of no help. I had to take control of the situation. "Does anyone come to check on us?"

He gave a quick nod. "Twice. They didn't enter the cell. Just peered through the bars. Maybe they're waiting for you to awaken."

I rose and moved to the cell door. Gripping the lock, I gave it a vicious yank. It didn't budge.

High-pitched laughter spilled from his mouth. "Don't you think I tried that already?"

Turning it in my hand to inspect it, I responded, "Now I'm trying it."

"You're wasting your time. It's a prison. There's no way out."

I chose to ignore his whining, trying instead to garner more information. "How many hunters are there?"

He lowered his chin to his chest. "Too many."

"Give me a number, Osiris!"

He sneered at me. "Maybe twenty."

I knelt down and rested my hand on his knee. "Earlier this evening, The Ten killed nine hunters."

"Nine...nine are dead?"

I gave a slight nod, employing a sidelong glance down the cells on the right wall and then the left. All empty. I had to ask. "Where are Isis and Hathor?"

He stared right through me and swallowed hard. "I don't know.'

If this was in fact a vampire prison, where were the vampires? Osiris and I couldn't be the only ones, and it didn't make sense for them to hold only Osiris. Isis and Hathor had to be safe, and I wouldn't let my brain imagine the unthinkable. Despite the cruelty they inflicted upon me and the years of torment I endured, I could never wish such a fiery, painful death on any one of them. I pushed the grim thoughts from my mind and centered on Osiris. "What's the last thing you remember?"

He frowned as he struggled to recall the memory, and pushed on his temples as if that would help. "We stopped at a bar for a glass of wine, and…." He beat his fist against his forehead in frustration. "Then, I woke up in this hellhole swarming with hunters."

"So, Isis and Hathor were with you at the bar?" I probed.

His face contorted in pain. "Yes."

"Why didn't you summon The Ten? One mental message from you and they would have come running to help."

"Shame." He briefly met my eyes then looked away. "Isis and I got caught up in Hathor's obsession with Amon. Her constant sniveling manipulated us." He dropped his head into his hands, and a shudder ran through him. "Those are mere excuses. The truth is, all three of us are responsible for your suffering and Amon's suffering. To die at the hands of hunters seemed a just punishment."

This wasn't the time or the place to dredge up past wrongs. Dwelling on any of that would be of no assistance whatsoever. At best, it was a hindrance to our current situation. I tried instead to focus on the positive. "Isis and Hathor have to be here. We'll find them."

He pointed to the padlock. "How are we going to do that, Beth?"

"Amon will track my blood." I took his hand and squeezed it. "It will lead him here. The Ten will come for us. But until they do, we have to be clever. Make no mistakes. Show no emotion. Don't let them get under your skin."

"Easy for you to say; you haven't suffered their torture techniques yet."

The heavy thump of combat boots striking the cement drove us to opposite corners. Rising to my feet, I pushed my shoulders back and let my arms hang loose at my sides.

A tall figure emerged under the unnatural glow of the fluorescent lights. A thin layer of sweat coated my palms. With a quick swipe down my jeans, I erased this evidence of shaky nerves.

The figure hugged the back wall, staying in the shadows cast by the lights. *Silly fool. My vampire eyes show me all.* As my sight zoomed in closer, my assailant came into view. His carrot-red hair sent a shiver down my spine. Danny.

He stepped into the light, facing the cell. He took a wide stance and clasped his hands behind his back like a soldier. "Well, well, well...what do we have here?"

I wanted to slap the smug smirk off his freckled face, but I stood completely still, offering him a playful grin. "Danny, what's this all about?"

"Y-y-you know him?" Osiris stuttered.

Danny jutted a finger at Osiris. "No one's talking to you." He jerked his head back toward me. "I'll tell you what this is about...ridding the world of bloodsuckers like you."

I shrugged, as if his threat didn't bother me in the least. "So, I'm your prisoner?"

His greenish-blue eyes grew tremendously dark, more so than I would have imagined they could. "Damn right you are."

Standing as tall as I could and freeing my voice of any emotion, I stated, "I demand my freedom."

Danny crossed his arms and huffed, "Hell no. You can kiss your vampire ass goodbye."

So much rage was bottled up inside him. I had to defuse it some-how. I took a step closer to the bars. "Look at me. I'm the same girl you grew up with, fell in love with."

He violently shook his head. "That girl is gone. I'm staring at a monster."

"Me? *You* shoved a needle in my neck and drugged me."

He didn't flinch, beg for forgiveness, or lower his gaze. "And I'd do it again. You're not human. You made a choice to end your human life."

Anger stole my emotional control. I raised my voice to a supernatural pitch. "NO, I DID NOT." I shut down, not saying another word, gathering self-control. In a much calmer tone, I continued. "I was shot, bleeding to death. I was scared. I didn't want to die. So, I guess I didn't have much of a choice. I could have chosen to die, but I chose to live."

Danny's mouth fell open and for a moment, he didn't speak. I thought maybe I had him, but despite my explanation, the flat, soured expression flooded back. "How you became what you are is irrelevant. You feed off humans. You drink their blood." His lips curled back from his teeth as if the sight of me disgusted him. "Your kind kills people. That's sick and immoral. It has to end. *You* have to end."

His ominous stare, the disgust in his voice, and his rigid body said it all. I could tell he meant every word. I glanced at the proof of Osiris crumpled on the floor, unable to stand. I dug my nails into my palms. "Will you torture me too? Is this what has become of you, a malicious, bitter thug?"

"You have no right to judge me." His mouth twisted into an ugly snarl. "You're the killer."

"And you're not one?"

Beads of shiny sweat lined his forehead. He stabbed a finger through the bars at me. "I can't kill what's already dead."

I spread my arms and turned in a circle. "Do I look dead to you? We feel pain, hurt, joy, guilt, and love." I searched his eyes, hoping to find a glimmer of mercy. "Our emotions are a thousand times stronger than any human's."

His nostrils flared as a bright flush spread across his cheeks. "I'll never sanction what you are or the despicable things you do." He raised his voice. "So stop trying to sway me."

I shook my head, saddened by his hate. "How did you get mixed up in all this, Danny?"

His eyes bugged. "You should know. The only girl I ever loved walked away to be with a vampire. It ruined my life. *You* ruined my life."

I lowered my gaze. "I never wanted to hurt you, but there are things you don't know. Things about my past." I lifted my head, my eyes meeting his accusing ones.

He laughed at me. "It's too late. I don't care anymore. I came to London to join the hunters. They accepted me. They gave me purpose." He moved to walk away. "It's been swell catching up with you, Beth, but I've got places to go and vampires to fry."

I rushed forward, gripping the cold metal bars between my fingers. "Wait!"

Danny sighed heavily. "What?"

"The two vampires that were with him." I gestured toward Osiris. "Where are they?"

Osiris raised his head, his gaze fixed on Danny.

Danny raised his brows and smirked. "Oh, you mean the one who thinks she's God's gift to man, and the other who believes she's Cleopatra?"

Osiris grabbed onto the bars, hoisting himself up and shaking a threatening finger at Danny. "If you harm them, I'll..." His wobbly legs buckled, and he plopped down with a thud.

Danny doubled over, laughing and holding his ribs. "You'll what, crawl after me?" Waving a dismissive hand and turning his back on us, he stomped away.

Tightening my fists around the bars, I shouted after him at the top of my lungs, "Danny, if I *ever* meant anything to you, if you *ever* loved me, please, release the female vampires. They're his family...please."

Danny came to a grinding halt, clenched his fists, and then stormed off.

Osiris wailed into his palms, "Isis."

I rushed to his side, dropped to my knees, and put my arm around him. "He won't hurt them." I noticed my voice lacked conviction. The Danny I knew was gone, and I had no idea what the new Danny was capable of.

Osiris latched onto my arm. "She's everything to me. I can't survive without her. She's my life."

Not knowing what else to say, I repeated my words. "He won't hurt them."

The scuff of boots accompanied by a strange scraping against the concrete floor grew closer in my ears. I left Osiris's side to peer through the bars. Three men clothed in camouflage gear trudged toward us, dragging two individuals by their arms. Danny followed, bringing up the rear. Their prisoners, trying to crawl along on their hands and knees, struggled to keep up with the steady march of the men. Their gray-tinted flesh and muddy clothes sent me back a step. With one blink and a refocus I knew. The blonde and black–haired females were un-mistakable. I ran to Osiris, dragging him to the front of the cell. "Look! It's Isis and Hathor. Danny brought them to us."

He sagged against me, crying tears of relief.

As they neared the cell Danny came forward, raising a bow armed with a flaming arrow. "Get away from the door, Beth."

I didn't hesitate to shuffle backward, keeping Osiris close at my side.

One of the men approached the door, his eyes glued on me. With a flick of his wrist he unlocked the padlock, then swung the door open. The other two men restraining Isis and Hathor lugged them forward and pitched them inside the cell, like they were tossing out garbage. The pair scrambled to the far edge of the cell, huddling together, shivering.

After snapping the lock closed, the three men ambled up the hall, clapping each other on the back and thrusting their fists into the air, hooting and hollering like frat boys.

Danny snuffed out the flames and lowered the bow and arrow. He kept his gaze fixed on me. I took my eyes off him to glance back at Isis and Hathor. Locked in each other's arms, their stricken, gaping eyes told a story of absolute terror.

Osiris crawled over to them, reaching out his hand. His tone drip-ping with devotion, he said her name. "Isis."

Her eyelashes fluttered before she slowly rolled her head to look at him. A blank stare emanated from her ashen, sunken face. Hathor nudged her, snapping her out of her daze. Isis blinked, then her eyes grew wide. A gasp flew from her lips, and she stretched out her arms. "Osiris."

Flinging their arms around each other, they clung to one another, sobbing.

Hathor sat stiff and still, tears streaming down her shriveled face. Osiris grabbed Hathor's hand and pulled her into their embrace. He glanced up at me and whispered, "Thank you."

I centered my attention back on Danny. "Look at them. Do you see monsters?"

At that moment an ear-piercing shriek echoed through the hallway, the high-pitched sound bouncing off the walls. Danny shuffled backward, grabbing up the bow and arrow and aiming it toward the sound. "What the hell was that?"

A series of chills ran over my skin. *Oh God, The Ten.* "Danny," I screamed, "come inside the cell. You have to hide. Hurry!"

He ignored me, peering deeper down the darkened hallway.

The sickening snap of bones breaking resounded in my ears. Primal screams of terror followed by the pounding of boots against the cement thundered toward us. Gripping the bars and shaking them to no avail, I cried, "Danny, please get inside the cell."

The tendons stood out in Danny's neck, and his pulse became visible with the strength of his fear. He turned toward the cell, a look of complete horror draining the color from his face.

Stomping my feet and frantically waving him over, I shouted, "Now, damn it!"

Hunters barreled into the hallway, eyes bulging in fear, knocking Danny to the floor. His mouth flew open, and a monstrous cry bellowed from him as chaos erupted all around him. A whoosh of cold air passed the cell, and then another and another; The Ten relentlessly pursuing the men at speeds not even my eyes could detect. Hunters bolted out of hiding, scattering in all directions, slamming into one another and striking blindly, inevitably taking some of their comrades out in their fear. Some of them just sank to the ground, blubbering and throwing their hands up in surrender. The Ten whirled overhead like angry hornets, plucking hunters off their feet and breaking their necks in midair. Screaming, wailing, and moaning came at me from all sides, causing the hair to lift on the back of my neck. *Not Danny, please not Danny.* I skimmed every face, searching for his. Not a trace of his orange hair or his freckled skin fell into my line of vision. I pounded my fists against the cell door, struggling to be heard over the screams. "Amon, protect Danny. Spare his life!"

Fingers surrounded my ankle, tugging hard enough to pull me backward. Osiris knelt beside me, clinging to my ankle with a death grip. "Get out of the line of fire. You must wait this out. Amon will do what's best."

I shrank down next to him, dropping my head into my hands, and he wrapped his bony arm around my shoulder. Squeezing my eyes shut, I repeated the same words over and over again inside my head, willing them into being: *Let Danny live. Let Danny live. Let Danny live.* Somewhere around the fiftieth time, I realized my inner voice was the only sound in the now-quiet prison. I let my mind go blank, silence surrounding me. I felt Osiris's arm still draped across my shoulder. Isis and Hathor crept up to sit on either side of him.

Footsteps approached. Rising to my feet, I strained to see into the dark. Striking emerald-green eyes shimmered from the dimly lit hallway.

"Amon," I called out, rushing to the door of the cell.

"Beth," his angelic voice sang out.

His handsome face finally emerged into the light. Weakness consumed me, and I slumped against the bars. Hot tears burned at the corners of my eyes as I locked my gaze on my love. He and Horus led the pack, with Nephthys, Ptah, Anubis, and Kuhn on their heels. Sobek brought up the rear, his arm locked around Danny's neck as he hauled him forward.

"Thank God," I uttered. I'd lost my best friend, Anna, at the hands of a vampire. I couldn't bear to lose Danny too, no matter what he'd done or what he'd become. I'd do anything in my power to save him, anything.

Amon hastened his stride, launching across the cement and gripping the lock in the palm of his hand. He curled his fingers around the evil device, squashing it like an overripe grape. Bits and pieces crumbled to the floor, dusting his shoes with the tiny specks of metal that remained. He threw the door open, and I rushed into his arms, kissing him as if we'd spent years apart.

I let my lips linger on Amon's just a bit longer before pulling away to face Danny. The puzzled gaze gripping his face called for an explanation. "Like I told you, there are things you don't know."

Horus and Nephthys charged into the cell, dropping to their knees and embracing the previously lost trio. They clung to one another, every shoulder quaking with their sobs.

Horus kissed Isis's cheek and murmured, "Mother."

Nephthys snuggled up to Isis, smoothing her hair.

"Who the hell is that guy?" As an afterthought, Danny chimed in, his tone thick with bitterness, "What happened to that vampire you left me for?"

Amon assessed Danny's face, recognition lighting his eyes. "You're the boy who called me Commander Vapor."

Danny eyed Amon up in disbelief. "You're the mist."

Amon bowed theatrically. "That I am." He arched a brow at Sobek. "Let him go, Sobek. He's not going anywhere."

Sobek tightened his grip instead. "We can't let him go. Look what he's done." He inclined his head toward the vampires embracing on the cell floor. "He must be destroyed."

Danny struggled in Sobek's grasp. "Get off me, you brute."

I bolted forward, clenching my fists in rage. "You will *not* harm him."

Sobek grunted at me like some barbaric caveman. "I don't need your approval."

I spun, appealing to Amon. "Don't let this happen."

Amon approached Sobek with his arms spread wide in amity. "Sobek, you alone cannot decide this human's fate."

Sobek shoved Danny forward. "Who wishes to see this worthless mortal pay for what he's done? I know I would."

Anubis spoke up first. "I."

Khum followed suit. "I."

Horus raised his hand. "I."

Nephthys gave a firm nod. "I."

"What's wrong with all of you?" I shouted as I pointed at Osiris, Isis, and Hathor in the corner of the cell. "The three of them said nothing, because it was Danny who reunited them. You can't just kill someone because you feel it's appropriate. None of you can."

Anubis huffed out a breath stubbornly. "We've been doing it for centuries."

"No. You're governed by the blood lottery," I corrected him. "The Council tells you when you are allowed to take a life."

Spots of color appeared in Danny's cheeks. "Stop defending me. I don't need your pity."

"This isn't pity." I went to him and ran my hand along his cheek. "I care for you."

An ugly scowl consumed his face. He jutted his head forward and spit in my face. "Go to hell."

Amon roared in rage as he backhanded Danny across the face, knocking him to the ground several feet away. "You're lucky she cares. I do not. *They* do not."

Danny groaned, slowly rising to his feet, rubbing his already-darkening cheek.

I hung my head, wiping Danny's saliva off my face. He hated me, truly hated me. I couldn't blame him. I'd wronged him, done this to him. This was my fault. If only I could go back in time and reverse my mistakes. I would have never let our friendship evolve into boyfriend and girlfriend. He'd loved me in a way I could have never returned. My heart had always belonged to Amon, and I realized that fully now in a way I never had before. No matter what else I'd tried to convince myself of, it always had and always would. Changing the past I couldn't do, but somehow, someway, I had to change Danny's future.

Amon pulled me close into his side, whispering into my ear, "Stop blaming yourself. This isn't your fault."

I took his hand and leaned against him. How kind of him to try and take away my guilt, but he was wrong. This *was* my fault.

"Danny's fate is not in our hands," Ptah announced, scraping his hand over his beard. "The Council must decide. We will bring him before them."

Anubis nodded his assent. "Works for me."

"Me too," Nephthys said, after receiving a nudge from Isis.

Horus agreed as well. "I accept this."

Khum looked at Sobek and raised his brows. "Fair enough, Sobek?"

Sobek pursed his lips and folded his arms across his chest. "I don't like it. He's tortured our comrades, killed several of our kind." He raised his eyes to me and thrust his hand in my direction. "Kidnapped Beth. He laid the path for his own destruction."

"Sobek," Osiris protested in a firm tone. "Leave this to The Council."

He grunted in frustration. "Very well. I will comply; but let it be known, I do not agree," he said with a hard edge to his voice.

"Understood," Osiris acknowledged before turning his attention to Danny. "Tell them where you store the blood. We're starving, and right now the only option for a meal is you."

Danny's eyes widened and there was a quake in his voice when he spoke. "We keep the blood in a small refrigerator in the room at the end of the hall on the right."

Sobek dashed off, vanishing down the hallway, and returned bearing an armful of blood bags. Bending before Osiris, Isis, and Hathor, he smiled warmly as he handed four bags to each of them. "Drink, my friends."

Their shaking, skeletal hands ripped at the plastic, spattering blood across their faces. The first two bags were downed without a breath taken. Their eyelids hung heavy, consuming the third. By the time the fourth bags were consumed, their bodies transformed one frame at a time, like flipping through a picture book. The beautiful sheen of their flawless skin was restored, as well as the brilliant hue of their eyes and rich silkiness of their hair. They rose from the ground as one, holding their heads high, appearing as powerful gods once more. Hathor turned her head, finding Amon's icy stare. She dropped her chin to her chest, pulling her long golden locks over her face. Osiris and Isis approached the cell door.

Amon lunged out, snatching Isis by the arm. "No magic." His eyes burned into her, his tone thick with threat. "You must face The Council for your crimes."

She glared at his hand, which secured her arm in a way that offered no hope of escape. "We have no intention of eluding The Council, Amon. Hathor, Osiris, and I will go willingly with you to their haven."

He didn't release her. Osiris came forward, placing his hand on Amon's shoulder. "We're ready to face The Council, Amon." Osiris's eyes slid in Hathor's direction. "All of us."

Sobek slapped Danny on the back none too gently. "Don't forget about this one."

Danny grumbled, "As if *I* have a choice."

"Better get moving," Anubis said, snapping his fingers. "We have just enough time to make it to the haven before sunrise."

I clutched at my arms as a flutter of nerves gripped my stomach. I couldn't focus. Mental numbness had set in. Amon's return, Philippe's betrayal, murderous hunters, Danny's hatred, and at long last finding Osiris, Isis, and Hathor. My emotions had been kicked into overload. For a young vampire of five years, these events measured up to a lifetime of change. Revenge no longer darkened my heart against Osiris, Isis, and Hathor. Their bleak, tortured, frail appearance when I'd first found them outweighed any punishment The Council could dish out. And the gory images of the hunters' broken, bloodstained bodies would be forever etched into my brain.

My only comfort in all of this had been Amon's return. Since I'd been a very young girl I'd loved him, or the mist I'd known to be him, with that heart-wrenching love nothing or no one could derail. Danny and Philippe had tried, and I'd even fooled myself into believing I'd loved them, but now, with Amon at my side, I knew what I'd felt for them both was a substitute for love. I'd wanted desperately to experi-ence any form of love that could fill the crater carved out from deep inside my heart. Danny and Philippe had every right to condemn me to a world of misery after I'd abandoned them both, attempting to fulfill my own selfish needs, and so I understood and accepted their anger and betrayal. However, even though I'd made my choice, I couldn't walk off into that hypothetical sunset with Amon just yet. The Council an-ticipated our arrival, at which time the fates of Danny, Osiris, Isis, and Hathor would fall into their hands.

CHAPTER 10

We entered The Council's haven single file, like prisoners or the most dismal school children in the world. Adam, Dinah, and Miriam stood just inside the threshold. Their cold, dead eyes was not the welcome I'd hoped for, but I was not their focus. The wayward trio guided their line of vision. Adam and Dinah approached Osiris, Isis, and Hathor. The three defiant gods were whisked away through the stone arch on the far left. Without saying a word, they disappeared down the dark passageway. Miriam stayed behind to lead the rest of us into the circular foyer. She turned and held her hand up in front of her, like a school crossing guard. "Wait here. I will inform Kohath of your arrival." She too vanished into the darkness of the same passageway.

I leaned over and whispered in Amon's ear, "Danny's human. He has no place here. The Council shouldn't be deciding his fate."

In a hushed voice he responded, "He's a vampire killer. Who else but The Council should judge his crimes?"

I couldn't come up with a reply. He had a valid point, but vampires deciding a human's fate? How could they be impartial? They perceived humans as food, survival, a means to an end. I felt it was just wrong, but what did my opinion matter? I had no seat on The Council, but when it came to Danny's fate, I'd make damn sure my voice was heard. Pushing my feelings about the subject deep down inside, I skimmed the foyer with my eyes, a strange feeling of déjà vu creeping into my bones. Not one piece of furniture claimed a place in the room. The teardrop chandeliers and gold ceilings gleamed as if brand new. Vibrant green foliage tumbled down the staircase, spilling onto the marble tiles like a waterfall. Modernization seemed prohibited within the haven's walls; even The Council dressed in centuries-old cloaks and gowns. Maybe change wasn't in their nature, or perhaps they simply refused to let go of their royal entitlement. And there I was, with tangled, rainwater-soaked hair, muddy boots and skinny jeans, and a torn and filth-streaked sweater.

Truly we all came across haggard and worn, except Danny. He looked around, wide-eyed and slack-jawed, as if this was the coolest place ever instead of his possible execution chamber, which I would prevent at all costs.

The familiar sound of slippers brushing the stone floor echoed inside my ears. A flutter ran through my stomach, and Amon slipped his hand around my waist to pull me close. Why was I nervous? This wasn't about my fate. This concerned Osiris, Isis, Hathor, and Danny. Was I worried for Danny? Of course, I was. If I had one focus today, it would be to save his life.

The Council's jewel-like eyes glowed in the darkness of the passageway as they neared our party collected under the stone arch. Hypatia was among them, beautifully dressed in a full-length light-colored gown, walking into the room with that same crestfallen stride. Statuesque and angelic, The Council entered the foyer, forming a single row to face us. Hypatia stood just behind The Council, her eyes on the ground. Adam and Dinah returned to take their place in line, as did Miriam. Teresa strode out of the passageway on the opposite side, her chin raised in confidence and Philippe at her side. Caleb, Margarete, and Jaffa followed. They approached The Council and stood to their right. Kohath gave Hypatia a gentle smile and motioned for her to stand by his side.

My attention drifted toward Teresa and Philippe. They stood side by side, their arms brushing in what seemed to be a deliberate manner. A warm glow lit Teresa's pallid cheeks, and Philippe kept stealing glances at her. Was something going on between the two of them?

Danny snapped his head in Philippe's direction. Staring defiantly at the powerful vampire who'd been my husband, he shouted, "You! You're the one. You stole Beth from me."

Philippe's gaze darted back and forth between Danny and me. He opened his mouth to speak, but must have thought better of it, clamping his lips together tightly.

Kohath broke formation and strode over to Danny. He held Danny in his sights, staring long and hard, locking their eyes and entering his mind. Danny stood motionless, his arms loose at his sides, his eyes glazed over, and his mouth slack. Kohath reverted his gaze, released Danny, and then turned his attention to The Ten.

Danny growled at Kohath with menace in his voice. "Did you just get inside my head, vampire?"

Kohath glanced at him with an unmistakable flash of authority, putting Danny in his place and letting him know where he ranked in the scheme of things. In a tone matching his look, Kohath stated, "That I did." He turned away from Danny once more, faced The Ten, and folded his hands behind his back. "Hunter or not, a human has no business being here."

I nudged Amon and whispered, "Exactly my point."

Amon frowned and gave me a sidelong glance.

"I suggested bringing him here," Ptah offered. "Otherwise, Sobek would have killed him."

Kohath raised his thick flaxen brows at Sobek.

"Don't look so surprised, Kohath." Sobek folded his arms across his chest. "I've killed many hunters. What's one more?"

"This is the twenty-first century, Sobek," Kohath pointed out. "We no longer behave like barbarians."

"It is the hunters who are barbaric," Anubis challenged.

Horus jerked his head toward Danny. "He tortured my mother and father. And Hathor, your maker. How can you not be troubled by his actions?"

In a gentle tone, Kohath said, "Revenge is never the answer, no matter the catalyst."

Danny stared blankly as if none of this mattered. Perhaps he just couldn't be bothered with whether he lived or died.

Nephthys approached Kohath and tossed her hair over her shoulder. "I could care less about him. But I demand to know what you've done with Isis."

Horus followed suit. "Yes, and Father too. Where are they? I want to see them."

Kohath's overbearing stare bore down on Nephthys and Horus before he responded. "Five years ago, those three took matters into their own hands, defying a decision made by The Council. This matter must be addressed. Does this not trouble you, Horus?"

Nephthys latched onto Horus's arm in stilted silence.

"What will you do with them?" Horus asked, his tone grim.

"Tonight, The Council will gather and decide their fate. You both may testify on their behalf."

Nephthys spoke up eagerly. "Yes, yes, of course I will."

"As will I," Horus declared.

Kohath turned from them, closing the conversation on the fate of the three fugitives for the moment. "The decision at hand for now is this man's fate."

"Kill him," Sobek roared, pumping his fist in the air.

Khum mirrored his comrade's view on the subject. "The hunter must die."

Anubis, completely self-absorbed, smoothed a few stray hairs, straightened his scarlet tie, and without so much as a glance in Danny's direction, rattled off, "Kill him."

Danny didn't help his case by muttering, "If you let me live, I'll just keep hunting you."

My jaw dropped. What the hell was wrong with Danny? Did he have a death wish or something? I refused to stand there and let this nonsense continue.

"This is ridiculous. You can't just kill him. Wipe his memory clean or give him new ones, but murder cannot and will not be an option."

Danny scowled at me. "Stay out of this, Beth."

Kohath's expression changed, a smile brightening his face. "Beth, that is a brilliant idea." He whirled to face his line of members. "Miriam, take Danny to one of the slumbering cellars. I will join you there shortly."

Miriam nodded, "Of course."

Grasping Danny's arm, she attempted to pull him forward. He resisted, planting his legs far apart and jerking his arm away. "I'm not going anywhere with you."

She eyed him up and down, and then offered him a becoming smile. "I can compel you to come with me or you can come with me of your own accord. It's up to you."

He clenched and unclenched his hands in rage. Twisting his head over his shoulder, he glared at me and snarled. "I'll get you for this, Beth. I swear I will." He faced Miriam and barked out, "Let's go."

She slipped her arm under his and ushered him out of the foyer and down the same passageway Adam and Dinah had taken the other three prisoners.

The crushing weight of Danny's words sliced through my gut like a knife, but I refused to allow my pain to turn to hate. I'd broken him, so I had to save him in any way I could.

Amon came up behind me and wrapped me inside his arms. "He'll be okay, Beth."

I didn't share his optimism. I'd have to see how it all played out; then and only then would I relax.

Kohath clasped his hands in front of him and addressed the group. "Once again, two emotionally charged matters have been placed before The Council. Neither calls for an easy resolution. We will reconvene this evening. In the meantime, we have prepared rooms for our guests. For everyone's comfort, we have left a bottle of our finest wine in each room, something to help take the edge off your troubled minds." He bowed his head. "A Council member will escort you all to your rooms. Rest well."

The Council members dispersed, Athaliah drifting past the others to make her way over to me and Amon. Her long blonde hair swung across her face, but it failed to completely hide that wild gleam dancing in her navy-colored eyes.

"Wait," Hypatia called out.

I turned toward her.

Kohath stopped as well, his gaze falling on Hypatia. "They need rest, Hypatia," he said. "Whatever you have to say can wait until nightfall."

She disregarded his remark, her gaze on me. "We must speak."

Kohath smoothed her hair in an attempt to calm her. "Let me take you to the slumbering cellar. I can have one of the scholars stay with you until I can return to you."

In a fashion of pure defiance, she shook her head. "No. I am not your possession, Kohath. Stop acting as such and leave me be. It is Eeth I wish to speak to."

We had one brief encounter on a sea-cliff bench. What could she possibly need to speak with me about?

Kohath exhaled a defeated breath, stepped back, and then said, "Very well."

Hypatia turned to Athaliah. "Give us some space."

"Of course," she said, edging backward and toward Kohath.

Amon held his ground, sticking by my side.

Hypatia waved him away. "You too."

Before he made any attempt to retreat, he looked at me.

"It's okay," I assured him.

He left my side and claimed a spot next to Kohath and Athaliah.

With the others a safe distance away, I spoke. "I don't understand. What it is you think I can do?"

She took my arm and steered me several more paces to the left, creating isolation from the others. Her eyes took on a magnificent and powerful blaze. "More than you know."

"What do you mean? How does that involve me?"

"Not here," she whispered, dragging me all the way to the far corner of the foyer. "I am here against my will. I must escape."

I leaned closer in and kept my tone low. "Are you saying they apprehended you?"

Her eyes darted about before she answered. "Yes. I fear this time I will not find a way out."

"This time?" I caught those words.

"I have been captured and escaped these walls time and time again. My brother has concern in his heart for me. Believes I am a danger to myself and others, and now I am guarded like a criminal. I won't make it out of here again."

"Has Kohath forbidden you to leave?" It seemed rather harsh and against his benevolent nature.

A heavy sigh spilled out of her mouth. "I am not certain, but the guards...why else would I be guarded?"

"Hypatia!" I said her name with force. "How should I know? You're not making sense. We barely know each other. Why come to me?"

Tears glistened in her eyes and a shudder ran through her. "The child I spoke of has been born. His name is Brandon, and I have gazed into his eyes and witnessed the soul of my true love inside this tiny human being." She balled her fists and bared her fangs. "The Council keeps me from the infant for fear I will harm him." Her fingers relaxed and her whole body seemed to sigh. "How could they think this of me? I love him. I could *never* let any harm come to him."

Again, I questioned. "Why me?"

Her eyes burned into mine and she went off on a rant. "They have demanded I give him up, stating the boy is no longer rightfully mine. I begged my brother to undo this unjust sentence, but he refuses.

"Words cannot express the hopelessness I feel. Brandon's world will come crashing down on him, and he will need my guidance and comfort to endure the challenge and confusing time to come. I *will not* stand by and watch this play out." She joined our hands and gripped my fingers. "You ask why you? Amon is your lover, immortal companion, and a vampire god. If he were to sanction my request, The Council may reconsider."

I pushed away from her. "Manipulate Amon?" I eyed her up and down. "I won't do it."

She clasped her hands, squeezing so hard her knuckles grew white. "You know firsthand the torment and pain of being separated from the one you love. To find your way back, you would do anything, sacrifice anyone, and maybe even kill. I beg you now, help free me. I have finally found my love. He has returned to me. Let me go to him. I will promise anything, sign away my immortal life in my own blood if I have to, but I must go to this child, for he will need me."

She was right. I knew all too well the painful heartache of separation. I mulled over her words and renounced my decision. "I will speak to Amon and to Kohath."

Again, tears welled up inside her eyes, pooling in the corners. She knelt at my feet and breathed, "Thank you."

I waved Amon and Kohath over.

She sprang to her feet and slapped her hands against her cheeks. "Now?!"

I stared hard at her and pressed, "You want to leave, don't you?"

She quickly nodded.

"Then what better time than the present?"

Amon leapt across the floor in a single immortal step, Kohath seconds behind. A huff of impatience flapped Amon's lips. "What is going on?"

"Yes," Kohath demanded, with an exaggerated arm cross.

I exhaled a breath, reluctant to rehash the entire story. "It'd be easier if the two of you just read my mind."

They rushed forward like a pair of meddlesome twins, ransacking my brain. Kohath let go first, his head slowing twisting to face Hypatia. Amon lingered, scrutinizing each word a second time around. Shortly thereafter he released me, and he too confronted Hypatia. She refused to look at either of them, keeping her focus on me.

"Well?" I asked, probing them both for an answer.

Amon presented his palms in an upward fashion as he stated, "I'm hardly unbiased on the subject of lost love. I would allow her to leave, Kohath."

Kohath plastered an unreadable expression on his face. "I will base my decision on fact, not on loyalty."

Hypatia's eyes flew to Kohath, and she growled out the hate in her heart for him. "You're no better than Father."

He flinched and stumbled backward; her words had obliviously hit home. Righting himself, he reclaimed his kingly posture and held his head high. He came to her and joined their hands. As he looked upon her with genuine fondness, he said, "I would never treat you like Father did." He raised her hands to his lips and kissed each one. "Go to the boy. You have my blessing."

A stunned look fell across her face. She stood very still, but only for a brief second, and then leapt into his arms and threw hers around his neck. High-pitched shrieks came next, then tears, and finally uncontrollable laughter. She bombarded his cheeks with kisses. Releasing him, she softly said, "Thank you," and then bolted out the haven door with supernatural speed.

Kohath steered Amon and I toward Athaliah. "Go on now, get some rest." He walked away, slightly shaken, and without his usual grace.

"Come," Athaliah said. She didn't wait for a response, turning her back on us and heading for the stone arch closest to the stairway.

The memory of her stabbing my hand with the sterling dagger jolted me as it played back inside my brain. I flinched and rubbed my thumb over the center of my palm. She glanced over her shoulder at me as a bemused smile spread across her face. I returned her smile with the most insincere one I could muster. Did she enjoy inflicting pain? Did it amuse her?

"This way," she directed, taking us into the dark passageway, dimly lit by only a few scattered lanterns.

On the other side of the passageway was a long, carpeted hallway, with several doors on either side. Each door bore an antique brass sconce with a bulb that mimicked the burning flame of a candle. Athaliah led us deep into the hallway. As we approached its end, she veered right, stopping in front of one of the many doors. Though she pushed the door open, she lingered in the doorway, blocking our entrance. Her navy-colored eyes grew dark and narrowed. She crept closer, her gaze fixed on the two of us. Stretching her slender neck toward us, she sniffed the air.

I glanced questioningly at Amon. He shrugged, seemingly as confused as I.

Her eyes darted back and forth—as if she were collecting information and processing it like a computer—before she turned and walked away without a single word.

"What the hell was that?" I demanded of Amon, not really expecting him to have an answer.

His eyes pursued her up the hallway. "I have no idea."

"I think she was smelling us."

"Well, I can't fathom why," he responded, shaking his head.

After we entered the room, Amon headed straight for the bottle of wine on a silver tray in the center of a small table by the door. "I could go for a glass of wine. How about you?"

"Yes," I said in earnest. I happened to glance down at my clothes and pressed the sleeve of my sweater under my nose. "Maybe she smelled me. My clothes reek of mud and that musty cell; not to mention my dirty hair."

He popped the cork and picked up one of the glasses. Filling it halfway, he remarked, "Nonsense, you don't smell offensive in any way."

I kicked off my boots and looked around the room. On the opposite wall, beside a giant four-poster bed draped in silk, stood a large dresser and mirror. I hurried over to the dresser to examine my reflection. Other than a few strands of tangled hair and smudged patches of dirt on my face, my appearance wasn't as horrific as I'd imagined. That revelation aside, I searched for something to wear, jerking open drawers. "Nothing but gowns."

He chuckled. "They are stuck in the regal ages of the past." After handing me a glass of wine, he approached the blazing hearth in the center of the room and propped his elbow on the mantle. A strand of his jet-black hair fell against his face in a charming way. The fire crackled, and the mixed scent of burning wood and blood-red wine filled the room. "To us," he said, raising his glass.

My heart fluttered and weakness consumed me when thoughts of long ago, when I'd surrendered my soul to belong to him forever, flooded my mind. I raised my glass. "To us."

A slight grimace ruined his face. "Never thought we'd be back here."

I took a swallow of my wine and answered, "Feels like déjà vu At least this time it's not me under scrutiny by The Council. What do you think they'll decide?"

He shrugged his shoulders. "Hard to say, but you're not concerned about Isis, Hathor, or Osiris. You're worried about Danny."

I released a nervous, pent-up breath. "I'm just scared for him. What if Kohath screws up his head while trying to erase his past? I couldn't live with myself if something terrible happens. It will be my fault. He's one of my oldest friends, and what he felt for me did this to him."

He came to me and cupped my face in the palm of his hands. "Listen to me; Danny *chose* to join the hunters. He *chose* to kill. You had nothing to do with those bad choices."

"But I broke it off with him to be with you, and that sent him down this path."

He sighed heavily. "Stop torturing yourself. Couples break up every day. Most jilted lovers don't go join a group of killers to deal with their grief."

It did have a silly ring to it. "I suppose you're right. It's been a long few days. Maybe I just need some sleep."

He kissed me. "Then rest."

Another whiff at my sweater put sleep on hold. "I need a shower first." I headed into the bathroom and cracked the hot water.

From the other side of the door, he called out, "I'll take your clothes to the laundry."

An oversized bathrobe hung on the back of the bathroom door. Stripping out of my clothes, I let them fall to the floor before slipping into the robe. I scooped up my clothes, stepped just outside the doorway, and handed them over to Amon.

He tucked them under his arm and winked at me. "Be back in a bit."

I blew him a kiss before walking back into the bathroom surrounded by a fog of steam. The hot water was delicious against my dampened, chilled skin. I vigorously rubbed the cold from my arms, trying to scrub away the stink of Highgate Cemetery and Danny's vampire prison. I couldn't relax, despite the heat of the water, for tomorrow The Council would gather, and I would learn what had become of my closest childhood friend.

****

My stomach twisted into knots as I followed the others down the familiar hallway, where statues of mystical gods guarded each doorway. The lanterns at its end flickered, softly illuminating The Council's gathering chamber. The black door with gold trim stood open to us. Teresa, stationed at the entrance, passed out goblets of blood to the eager vampires as they arrived. Motioning for us to come forth, she said, "The Council is seated and awaiting your arrival. Please, come inside."

Horus, Nephthys, Anubis, and Ptah were first to enter and collect their goblets, followed by Margarete, Caleb, Philippe, and Jaffa...who, of course, refused her goblet. Amon and I crossed the threshold together. I had to fight the urge to swallow the contents of my goblet in one gulp. In The Council's eyes it would have come across as too undignified. With Amon at my side, we glided across the floor toward the empty chairs, holding our heads high like royalty.

The Council sat poised on their thrones of authority behind the long marble table. As I took my seat, I acknowledged Kohath with a slight dip of my chin. He returned the gesture, kindness in his olive-colored eyes.

"Everyone in this room is aware of the reason we have gathered today," Kohath stated, averting his eyes, now clouded by displeasure, to the three wayward vampire gods seated before him and the other council members. "Calling forth individuals to bear witness is irrelevant. Over the past five years we have gathered more than enough information to arrive at our decision. Your list of crimes is quite lengthy. To name a few: division of loyalties, the alteration of lives, destined immortal companions estranged, and The Council's binding ruling ignored and violated." He leaned forward, speaking slowly and emphasizing his words. "How plead you?"

With grace, Osiris approached The Council, hands clasped in front of him in a gesture of humility. "Isis and I allowed ourselves to be caught up in Hathor's obsession with Amon—"

Hathor bolted from her seat and shot a fierce look at Osiris. "Don't you dare place all the blame on me!"

Isis sprang to her feet. "Why shouldn't we blame you, Hathor? After learning of the promise, you came to me in hysterics, begging me to use my magic on Amon. I refused; yet relentlessly, you were at my ear, demanding I mend your broken heart. You wore at me, ceaselessly, until I finally gave in."

Hathor's eyes doubled in size before she fired back, "How typical of you to avoid any blame. Did you forget it was you who took offense to a vampire commoner binding with a god? As I recall, your exact words were, 'I'd rather burst in flames than witness Beth binding with Amon.'"

Amon reached over to lightly stroke my forearm in an attempt to take some of the sting out of her words. His attentiveness moved me but did little to soften the blow of her words. The harshness with which she spoke raged like fire over my cool skin. I raised the goblet to my lips, filling my mouth with blood and swallowing past the rather large lump in my throat. The blood's magic and Amon's tender touch swiftly diminished the pain she intentionally hurtled my way. Something deep inside me, and quite unfamiliar, wanted to lash out with some nastiness of my own, but as I opened my mouth, Anubis intruded into the conversation.

"I, for one, believe Isis. We have all witnessed Hathor playing the 'woe is me' card."

"Shut up, Anubis," Hathor snapped. "No one asked for your opinion."

He threw his hands up. "I'm just saying...."

Osiris gripped Isis's arm, pulling her backward to put some distance between her and Hathor. "Hathor, this started well before the binding ritual. You begged Isis for help, and we sympathized with you. Your suffering became ours. We were blinded by it. The spell's purpose was solely intended to win Amon's love. Nothing more."

Hathor rolled her turquoise eyes at him. "Osiris, you'd say anything to protect your wife."

Osiris jerked his head back and splayed his hand over his chest. "I most certainly would not. Where is this hatred coming from, Hathor?"

Nephthys couldn't contain herself and shouted, "My sister pitied you and only wanted to ease your pain. Take some responsibility."

Hathor spun around and faced The Council. Looking directly at Kohath, she challenged, "Are you paying attention? Isis disrupted the binding for her own reasons. I just happened to get what I wanted in the process. The spell benefited both of us."

Kohath pressed his lips together in a hard grimace. After a moment, he set his sight on Isis and inquired, "Is this true? Did you have ulterior motives when you placed the spell upon Amon?"

Horus leapt to his feet, replying in Isis's place. "My mother never stated such venom regarding Beth. The spell was intended to end Hathor's suffering, nothing more."

Hathor clenched her teeth and ground out, "You're a liar."

Kohath made an attempt to placate her. "Hold on, Hathor. I assure you, The Council will find the complete truth." Turning his attention to Horus, he stated, "Horus, I need to hear directly from Isis."

Isis immediately stated, "I crafted the spell for Hathor."

Kohath regarded Isis with suspicion in his eyes. "Your words reek of deceit." He rose and cast his gaze on The Ten, demanding, "Who of you had knowledge of this spell?"

No one spoke.

Turning to Athaliah, he ordered, "Spear their palms and read their blood."

Athaliah pushed her chair away from the table and hurried from the room. There was no doubt in my mind the purpose of her hasty exit could only be to retrieve her precious sterling dagger.

Out of the corner of my eye, I caught Jaffa leaving her chair and approaching Kohath.

"My job is done," she offered in a flat tone. "I located these fugitives. This bickering back and forth has nothing to do with me."

"Agreed," Kohath stated, placing his hand on her shoulder. "May I have a word?"

She seemed intrigued, her form taking on a brilliant glow. "Why, yes."

Kohath led her to the far corner of the room and began to engage her in conversation. I couldn't make out a single word. He kept his voice low and off the vampire radar. Kohath then stretched out his hand, and she accepted it. "Thank you for your assistance," Kohath said, speaking at a level I could plainly hear.

"Of course," she replied. "Until we meet again." She then turned and moved toward the door.

"Wait," I called out, sprinting across the room to come to a stop directly in front of her. "You're leaving?"

An enigmatic smile spread across her charred lips, and she nodded. "You don't need me anymore, baby vamp."

I wasn't sure how I felt about her departure. I'd gotten rather used to having her around. She was a friend—someone I valued—but our lives were lived at opposite ends of the world, and it appeared it was time for her to return to hers. "Amon and I have closure because of you. I wanted to say thank you."

She leaned forward and lowered her voice. "If you ever need me, you know where to find me." She didn't wait for a response. She left my side, continuing on her path, exiting The Council's chamber with no further hesitation.

I was still standing there staring at the empty doorway, etching her image into my brain, when Athaliah returned, pushing past me carrying her beloved dagger. A flash of gold caught my eye. Was that the binding goblet? I did a double take. Nestled under her arm was indeed the ancient goblet I'd drank from five years ago. Was it used for multiple purposes? A bad feeling pulled at my gut. I hurried back to Amon. Cupping my hand to his ear, I whispered, "Why did she bring that to *this* meeting?"

He studied her for several minutes, and then his eyes widened just a hair. He turned to me and said in a grave tone, "I think it has something to do with us."

I gripped his arm in alarm. "What? Why?"

Kohath's voice filled the room, offering Amon no chance to reply. We both sat back in our seats and faced The Council. "All of The Ten please rise." He turned to Athaliah and nodded. "Begin."

Gripping the dagger handle, she approached Osiris and demanded, "Show me your palm."

He obeyed.

She centered the tip of the blade on his palm and lanced his flesh. A line of blood crawled to the surface as she dragged the blade along. She peered closely at the crimson fluid, nearly pressing her nose against his hand and following the flow of blood. Abruptly, she stood upright and pursued her next subject, Isis, repeating the process. Athaliah drifted from palm to palm, stabbing Hathor, Nephthys, Horus, Ptah, Anubis, Sobek, Khum, and finally Amon before she returned to her seat, laying the dagger to rest on the table. In an unbiased tone, she stated, "Osiris, Isis, and Hathor collaborated together, crafting the spell. Nephthys and Horus had full knowledge of their plans. The remaining Ten were oblivious."

A scowl overtook Kohath's face as he looked down upon Osiris, Isis, Hathor, Nephthys, and Horus. "The five of you went behind The Council's back, conspiring together, with no regard for the consequences."

An admission of guilt never passed their lips. Together they stood, exhibiting no fear on their faces or in their body language of The Council's wrath. Did they doubt the inevitability of an unfavorable ruling? Perhaps they viewed their supremacy to be above The Council's rule of law.

Kohath's gaze softened somewhat, yet his voice remained stern. "We will take into consideration the extreme torture inflicted upon Osiris, Isis, and Hathor at the hands of hunters; however, punishment must be carried out." He turned to the members of The Council. "State your name and preference of sentence."

"Miriam: banishment from The Council, exclusion from the blood lottery, and revocation of status and privileges as one of The Ten."

"Athaliah: five years of solitary confinement, which is equal to the length of the spell.'

"Adam: five years of solitary confinement, which is equal to the length of the spell."

"Dinah: banishment from The Council, exclusion from the blood lottery, and revocation of status and privileges as one of The Ten."

"Cain: banishment from The Council, exclusion from the blood lottery, and revocation of status and privileges as one of The Ten."

"Peter: banishment from The Council, exclusion from the blood lottery, and revocation of status and privileges as one of The Ten."

"Luke: five years of solitary confinement, which is equal to the length of the spell."

"Japheth: banishment from The Council, exclusion from the blood lottery, and revocation of status and privileges as one of The Ten."

"Tamar: five years of solitary confinement, which is equal to the length of the spell."

"Daniel: five years of solitary confinement, which is equal to the length of the spell."

"Samuel: banishment from The Council, exclusion from the blood lottery, and revocation of status and privileges as one of The Ten."

As the punishments were stated and the repercussions of the sentences sunk in for the accused, gasps escaped their lips and hopelessness crept into their features. Nephthys, Isis, and Hathor huddled together, joining hands. Horus trembled at his father's side. Osiris gripped Horus's shoulder and lowered his grief-stricken eyes.

All eyes turned to Kohath. His vote would determine whether banishment would be the determined fate for the three, or if the vote would instead end up in a tie. His pause was painful.

"Kohath," Tamar pressed, "what say you?"

A troubled look crossed his face and nestled deep within his brow as he answered. "Five years of solitary confinement, which is equal to the length of the spell."

"We are left with a tie vote," Adam pointed out.

Amon stood and faced The Council. "May I speak?"

Kohath waved him forward. "Of course."

Amon addressed The Council, standing tall and pushing power into his voice. "I crave justice more than anyone in this room; however, banishment seems to me to be far too extreme a punishment. I have lived amongst these gods for centuries. They do not deserve such a harsh ruling."

Ptah joined Amon and stood at his side. "I concur. Banishment is not the answer."

Anubis, Sobek, and Khum left their chairs, surrounding Amon and Ptah. Anubis gestured to Sobek on his right and Khum on his left. 'We are united and share in our opinions; banishment would be far too cruel. It is also a fruitless endeavor; I could never comply with the ruling. Wherever they may be banished to, I would go to visit them. How could I not? I'm sure all of us would. We are in fact, *The Ten*."

"Anubis speaks the truth. We are united in godly blood. It cannot be separated," Khum stated stoically.

"Thank you," Kohath said, his expression filled with gratitude at their attempt to salvage the wrong doings of their allies. "Is there anyone who wishes to recant?"

They exchanged glances, uncertainty in every eye, as the idea of recanting a ruling was unprecedented. For a long while no one spoke, until a member with deep-set hazel eyes rose from his seat.

"Do you wish to change your sentence, Cain?" Kohath asked.

"I do," he replied with conviction. "The majority of The Ten strongly oppose banishment, and while it is not their decision to make, their requests have moved my heart. I will change my sentence to five years of solitary confinement, which is equal to the length of the spell."

"Very well," Kohath stated, rising and spreading his arms wide. "Though it is not unanimous, The Council has arrived at its decision." He leveled his gaze at the accused. "Osiris, Isis, Hathor, Nephthys, and Horus, you will, all of you, serve five years at the haven in solitary confinement."

Hathor slumped into Horus's arms and wailed, and Osiris wrapped his arms around them, pulling the pair into a close embrace. Isis and Nephthys clung to each other, their eyes bulging with fear.

To see them stripped of companionship saddened me. Five years lost. Even though all of time stretched out before them, I knew just how long that span of years could be. I knew the torment they faced, the loneliness, the pain. At least I'd had my friends around me. They would be utterly alone. "Kohath," I said, my voice just above a whisper.

His olive eyes found me. "Yes, Beth, is there something you would like to say?"

"Yes," I said, adding steel to my voice.

All eyes turned to me. I let their inquisitive stares fade into the background, even Amon's, setting my sight on Kohath. "While I have the utmost respect for The Council's ruling, five years is a long time. I know firsthand. Could they not be kept in confinement together?"

He rose from his seat to approach me. Gazing down at me with pride, he said, "You have a generous, forgiving heart, young Beth. I believe The Council would be very much inclined to accommodate such a noble request." He turned to his members for a response.

"Miriam, agreed"

"Athaliah, agreed."

"Adam, agreed."

"Dinah, agreed."

"Cain, agreed."

"Peter, agreed."

"Luke, agreed."

"Japheth, agreed."

"Tamar, agreed."

"Daniel, agreed."

"Samuel, agreed."

Kohath knelt in front of me and added, "Agreed."

I felt a weight lift from my shoulders. "Thank you."

"You're welcome." He returned to his throne and declared, "Peter, Samuel, and Daniel, please escort the sentenced ones to confinement."

The five were herded like sheep from the gathering chamber. A rush of relief escaped me in the form of a weighted breath. Finally, it was over.

"We have another matter to address," Athaliah announced.

Or not.

Amon hurried back to his seat and reached for my hand.

"Everyone, please take your seats," Kohath requested before questioning Athaliah. "What is this about?"

Her eyes darted toward Amon and I. "They are the root cause of all this mayhem."

Her unforgiving tone set my nerves on edge. Amon had been right; the goblet was meant for us.

"Go on," Kohath urged.

Her voice rose with excitement, became almost shrill, when she said, "The binding ritual must be repeated, and this time with blood straight from the heart."

I sprang from my chair and clenched my fists. "You can't be serious!"

Amon got to his feet much more slowly than I and calmly stated, "I'm certain she's not."

Dead calm rested on Athaliah's face. "I assure you that I am."

"You're not sticking that thing in my heart." I stretched my arm in the direction of the spot occupied by the dagger.

She pinched her index finger and thumb together. "It's just a tiny prick. The sting will be over in a second. And you will both heal."

Amon defiantly declared, "Absolutely not."

Philippe rushed to my side, standing in front of me as a shield. "Are you out of your mind? You could kill her."

Kohath held his hands up in a placating manner. "Calm down, everyone. Athaliah has performed this very ceremony time and time again. No one would be harmed. That being said, why do you believe this to be necessary, Athaliah?"

She didn't take her eyes off Amon and I as she answered. "The first binding ritual should have prevented any interference by the spell; nonetheless, it did not. Amon allowed a silly love spell to control him, and Beth still carries love in her heart for Philippe."

I glared at Amon and demanded, "What does she mean, allowed?"

A crazed look came into his eyes, and he blurted out, "Still?" He turned toward Philippe and curled his lips back in disgust.

Ptah and Caleb sped across the room, Caleb to haul Philippe back to his chair, and Ptah to corner Amon so that he couldn't charge Philippe.

Athaliah huffed impatiently. "Need I say more?"

"Hold on a moment, Athaliah," Kohath warned. "I've yet to evaluate the situation. I have questions of my own." He looked in my direction. "Beth, who holds the key to your heart, Amon or Philippe?"

I didn't hesitate. "Amon."

"Amon, who holds the key to your heart, Beth or Hath—"

Amon didn't allow Kohath to finish. "Beth."

Kohath shook his head before addressing Athaliah. "I don't see the need to pursue a second binding."

She fixed her intense glare on me. "Do you love Philippe?"

"I care for him," I answered.

"Have you ended your relationship with him?"

"Not completely, but I—" She did mean "divorced," didn't she?

She interrupted the flow of my words with her upheld hand and turned her attention to Amon. "Amon, did you not agree to *share* Beth with Philippe?"

He laughed when he said, "Well, yes, but she was married to him. I couldn't just—"

She cut him off as well, rattling off another question. "Have you made love to her yet?"

I couldn't have been more shocked by her words.

Amon slammed his hands down onto his chair's arms and shouted, "That is none of your damn business!"

"I'll take that as a no," she retorted sarcastically.

"Answer the question, Amon," Kohath insisted.

Amon's posture stiffened and he spoke with hesitancy. "No, we have not."

She smiled, quite satisfied with herself. "Kohath, I urge you to reconsider. These two clearly are not fully committed one to the other. Who's to say what other circumstance might arise to drive them further apart? And must I remind you, Kohath, the binding ritual was performed in order to spare her mother's life?"

He arched a brow in irritation. "I'm well aware, Athaliah. You have proven there is cause. I consent to a second, more intense ritual."

The room buzzed with excited chatter. I leaned forward in my chair, suddenly nauseous, and allowed my head to fall into my hands. Amon's lips touched my ear. "We will get through this."

I didn't respond. All I could think about was the evil dagger puncturing my chest and piercing my heart.

"Silence," Kohath ordered. "Athaliah must concentrate, so there must be the utmost quiet in the room. All but Amon and Beth are required to clear the room."

"Beth," Philippe called out.

My eyes found Caleb dragging him out the door. Margarete stood next to my chair. She bent and whispered into my ear, "I have seen this ritual performed. You will survive. As she pierces your heart, stare into her eyes, not Amon's. She has the power to numb your pain."

I gripped her hand in both of mine. "Thank you."

She stroked my hair, kissed my cheek, and hurried from the room.

Ptah knelt in front of me, resting his hands on my knees. His eyes bore into mine. "You can do this." He rose to his feet and embraced Amon.

"Ptah, you must leave the room," Kohath urged.

Ptah patted Amon on the back before regretfully exiting the room.

"It is best you remain seated," Athaliah said, now that we were alone. "I will start with you, Amon. Remove your shirt."

He complied, laying it over the back of the chair. His fingers gripped the chair arms and, peering straight ahead, he told her, "I'm ready."

The familiar wild gleam lit up Athaliah's eyes as she bent over him, resting the blade just over his heart. She palpated his chest with her fingertips while holding the goblet under the blade. Without hesitation she plunged the tip of the blade into his chest.

Amon's eyes flew open, and he grunted, like a wounded animal in pain. His entire body shuddered and then crumpled in on itself.

My heart raced, and I barely managed to hold back a scream. "Amon...talk to me. Are you all right?'

In a low, hoarse voice he managed, "I'm okay."

Athaliah withdrew the dagger from his chest. As she held the goblet to his wound, she said, "Almost done."

Oh God, I was next. Amon was a thousand times stronger than me. How could I, a human turned vampire such a small number of years ago, endure such pain?

"Heal his wound, Kohath, while I prepare Beth," Athaliah said.

Kohath speared his finger with his fang, drawing blood and spreading it over the wound in Amon's chest.

Athaliah scooted over to me. Adrenaline pumped through my veins as my breath came in short, panicked gasps. My entire being screamed for me to run and escape the dagger.

She laid her hand over mine and assured me, "You'll be fine; just keep your eyes on me."

Her words brought to mind Margarete's. *I won't look away, Margarete*, I promised inside my head.

"Remove your sweater, Beth."

My hands were shaking so badly, I fumbled with my sweater three times before finally working it over my head. It fell to the floor, but Athaliah scooped it up and laid it neatly over the back of the chair.

"I'm going to start now, Beth," she said, locking her eyes on mine.

Her fingers tapped my breastbone just above my bra strap. When she took her finger away, she placed the tip of the blade against my skin. I jumped at the icy touch of cold metal and switched my focus to her eyes.

I heard Amon say, "It'll be okay, Beth. I love you."

I didn't respond or look away from Athaliah. I prayed she really had the power to numb my pain. The blade pierced my flesh and began its descent. Beads of sweat exploded across my brow. My fingernails stabbed the fabric, imbedding themselves into the chair arms. The blade tunneled deeper, carving into my heart. The blade's pressure sucked all the air from my lungs. Twinges of relentless pain flared across my ribs.

I cried out, but the force of my scream only intensified the throbbing pain impaling my heart. Tears I had no control of spilled from my eyes and rolled down my cheeks. My body slumped forward, my heartbeat slowing, my limbs growing numb. Surely, I was about to die.

Abruptly, the pressure subsided. Life returned to my limbs, and the sweet sound of my heartbeat thumped inside my ears. The blade was out, and Athaliah now held the goblet to my chest. The smell of blood hung thick in the air. I could almost taste it on my tongue.

"Almost done," Athaliah said as she rubbed my hand.

I gave her a flimsy smile and rolled my head to the side to find Amon's emerald-green eyes staring at me.

He leaned over to kiss my lips, then pulled away and held me in his gaze. "Are you okay?"

I bobbed my head up and down, but truthfully, I felt like crap.

Athaliah pulled the goblet away and handed it to Kohath. It was she who punctured her finger to heal my wound. It seemed like she held it there for a very long time. Afterward, she handed me my sweater. It was a relief to slip it over my head and arms. I'd done it!

Athaliah dipped the dagger into the goblet, giving our collective blood a good stir. She handed it to me first. "Drink until I tell you to stop."

"I remember," I said, taking it from her. The first swallow was like nothing I'd ever tasted; like drinking from the earth, all of creation, life, the nectar of the universe. Power surged inside of me, commanding my immortal heart to truly awaken and beat with the strength of a love I'd never known before.

"Stop," she ordered, and ripped the goblet away, not allowing me the chance to disobey. Handing it to Amon, she said, "Drink until you finish the last drop."

He tipped his head back and drank...greedily, I might add. As he finished and lowered the goblet, Athaliah took it from him. She beamed at us. "It is done. Look at one another."

We turned toward each other, and the entirety of the room faded into the background. Only he and I remained. Yearning filled Amon's eyes, and he held out his arms. Euphoria bubbled up inside me as I fell into his arms and embraced him, laughing out loud. My fingers tingled with the need to touch him.

I grabbed his hand and pulled him forward, racing toward our room. Throwing open the door and peeling off clothes, we jumped into bed, giggling like teenagers. His hands caressed and kissed every inch of my pale skin. Every touch set an electric jolt through my body. I craved him inside me and couldn't wait a second more.

"Make love to me," I whispered in his ear.

He enfolded me into his body and gave himself to me as his lips played over mine. His touch sent shivers down my spine, igniting a fire within me that consumed all rational thought. My body swelled with pleasure as we became one. I moved with him, absorbed by his passion, seduced by it and entangled in it. With every caress and kiss, my desire grew stronger. I lost myself in his embrace as waves of gratification rippled through my body and I surrendered to the ecstasy of his love. I was complete, whole, and alive. We were finally free. When our lovemaking ended, we collapsed into each other's arms. As I memorized his face with my eyes, I knew. Never again would I doubt our love...or let anything or anyone come between us.

CHAPTER 11

I woke with a start and bolted upright. Amon reached for me and pulled me back down.

"What's wrong?" he asked.

"Danny," I responded. "I have to know what's become of him." I ran my hands through my hair and sighed. "With the verdict and then the binding ritual...I can't believe it, but I completely forgot about him. I have to go look for him."

He wedged his arm under me and laid his head on my breasts. "Stay in bed. Danny will be fine."

I laughed softly and stroked his head. "Probably, but I can't rest until I know for sure." I scooted away from him and off the edge of the bed, giving him a playful wink. "Wait in bed for me. I won't be long." Before he could object, I gathered my clothes off the floor, pulling them on as I flew out the door with supernatural speed.

I tied my hair into a ponytail as I trekked along, drawing on my vampire senses to seek Danny out. But when I sniffed the air, an overload of scents slammed into my brain, delicate floral perfumes, musky colognes, fire embers, aged parchment, red wine, and of course, an indulgent amount of tantalizing blood. My head spun, and I brought a shaky hand to my forehead. I wouldn't be using that sense to seek Danny out again. I shook off the haze and stumbled forward, having absolutely no idea where to look.

Philippe rounded the hallway corner, and I very nearly fled. I just didn't have the time or the patience to deal with him at the moment.

"Beth, I've been looking for you," he said, trotting up to me.

I waved him away. "Not now, Philippe. I have to find Danny."

Philippe pointed in the direction he'd just come from. "I just passed him in the foyer. Looks like he's on his way out."

My breath caught in my throat. "No," I cried, and hurried forward. "I have to see him." He couldn't leave, not yet. I had to know The Council hadn't completely scrambled his brains; that they'd given him peace, a new lookout on life, and rid him of all his hate and doom.

Philippe grabbed my arm, holding me there. "No, Beth, don't. Seeing you may trigger a memory The Council failed to remove."

I pushed past him. "Get out of my way. I have to see him."

He raced after me. "Then I'm going with you."

I didn't respond. As long as he stayed out of it, I didn't care where he was.

I made it to the foyer just as Danny's hand surrounded the doorknob. "Danny," I shrieked, more desperately than I'd intended. But seeing him walk out of my life flooded me with a backwash of human emotions I couldn't hold back.

He released the door and turned toward me. From his left shoulder hung a laptop case, and his right hand gripped the handle of a briefcase. He set both on the floor in front of him. The goofy smile, complete with adorable dimples, I'd grown accustomed to as a teenager spread across his freckled face. "Yes?" he responded, regarding me without a spark of recognition.

I ran up to him, stopping to stare into his greenish-blue eyes and taking in every inch of his face. Philippe shadowed me, his stance alert with readiness.

Danny asked, "Are you part of the trials here? I don't remember speaking to you for my research papers."

"Research?" I questioned.

He inclined his head toward the baggage he'd placed on the floor. "I've been here for several days working with you folks. I have to admit this facility is fairly well equipped for XP. Probably why no one here has lesions on their skin."

I scrunched my brows together, not understanding.

He must have picked up on my confusion, as he explained, "Xeroderma pigmentosum...the skin sensitivity to sunlight. The university received a healthy grant, and we're collecting data for trials."

Kohath appeared in the archway closest to the foyer. He glided across the floor to join us. "I see you have met Professor Meeks," Kohath stated with a proud smile.

My eyes darted to Danny. "You're a professor?"

He chuckled. "Yes, and I'm doing everything I can to find a cure."

A sob stuck in my throat. The Council turned Danny into a professor at a university. How had they accomplished that?

Kohath gestured toward the door. "The car is waiting, Professor Meeks. We certainly don't want you to miss your flight."

Danny nodded and scooped up his bags. "Of course." He extended his hand to Kohath. "Again, thank you for your cooperation with our research."

"It is I who should be thanking you." Kohath walked with him to the door, pulling it open for him.

"Danny," I called out, rushing forward and erasing the distance between us.

"Yes?"

I looked up at him, and in a small voice I asked, "May I give you a hug?"

Kohath and Philippe both looked as though they were prepared to haul me away, until Danny answered. "Of course. I understand what a hardship this condition is."

Standing on my tiptoes, I reached to put my arms around his neck, hugging him with all my might. He patted me on the back without reacting to the chill of my skin. He released me, waved goodbye, and then walked out of the door and my life forever.

As Kohath closed the door, I ran to him and hugged him as well. "How did you do it? How did you make so many changes to his life in such a short amount of time? Is he really a professor at a university? Is there really a grant? Are they researching that disease? Does he truly not remember me?"

"Hold on, Beth, let me answer before you overwhelm me with questions."

I made a zipping motion across my lips, a penitent expression on my face.

"The Council is well connected, and our reach spreads far and wide. We have collaborators and business partners around the globe; a few are specialized underground organizations which serve this very purpose. I simply called in a few favors and gave Danny a new life. We erased old painful memories and gave him new ones, and yes, he has no recollection of a past with you or any memory you ever existed. The Council carried out your request just as you asked."

Philippe took a confrontational stance, pursing his lips. "Sounds like you're playing God."

Kohath grinned with pride. "I most certainly am."

I ignored Philippe, taking Kohath's hands in mine. "Thank you. Thank you so much."

He patted my hand. "You're most welcome. I must be off. I'm expected in the blood lounge for a toasting ceremony. Good evening." He folded his hands inside his robe and exited the foyer with all the grace of a king.

I sighed with contentment and hugged myself. "I feel so good about this. Finally, I did something right."

Philippe touched my arm, and I looked up, meeting his eyes. "I've been waiting to speak with you. Can we go outside into the garden?"

At this point, nothing was going to bring me down off my little cloud of happiness, and if Philippe wanted to get the guilt of cheating on me off his chest, so be it. I gave him a polite smile and responded, "Why not?"

We traveled through the very passageway Hathor had led me down five years ago toward the garden overflowing with blood-red roses. Neither of us spoke as we strolled along the brick walkway toward the same marble bench. I neared the statue of the praying angel, transfixed momentarily by his frozen stare. "Five years ago, I sat on your bench, and here I am again. This time, please watch over me and protect me from any harm." I bowed my head in an attempt to offer credence to my words.

"Please sit down, Beth," Philippe called out, interrupting my moment.

I raised my head, glancing once more at the angel before sitting next to him. "Yes, Philippe," I sighed. I couldn't help being a little annoyed.

A grimace sullied his face as he growled out, "I've wanted to say this for a while now, but you were angry—and rightfully so—and weren't ready to listen. That night after The Gallery's opening, when you walked in on me with that woman, I was drunk as a lord. Still, I knew what I was doing."

I eyed him furtively. Not really what I'd expected to hear.

He continued. "You hurt me, and I wanted to hurt you. It was childish, yes, but I wasn't thinking with my head. I was thinking with my heart...and you'd broken it."

"Philippe—"

He cut me off. "Please, let me finish. I have to get it all out."

I gave him a subdued nod.

"Thank you. When you walked in and I saw the look on your face, it filled me with total satisfaction. In fact, I gloated over it."

I remembered well the words he'd thrust inside my head that night. Was he trying to piss me off? If so, it was working.

"But the next morning..." He paused and swallowed hard before continuing. "I felt like a total ass. I agonized over what I had done, and there was nothing I could do to take it back." A pained look crossed his face, and he softly shook his head. "I'm so sorry, Beth. You don't know how much. I don't deserve your forgiveness, and I'll understand if you don't want to accept my apology, but I am truly sorry. I loved you. I still do. Please, forgive me."

His words overwhelmed me, but in a good way. "Of course, I accept your apology. I'm sorry too."

He gasped with relief. "Thank you." Then he held up his hand. "Before you say it, I will. It's over between us. You love Amon, and your life is with him. I won't stand in your way."

I reached for his hand and squeezed it. "Thank you, Philippe."

He held onto mine a few seconds longer, and then let go. "I really do want you to be happy."

"I want you to be happy too." I gave him a playful nudge. "Does Teresa make you happy?"

He smiled like a teenage boy. "She's nice."

"And?" I pressed.

"And we'll see how it goes. She asked me to stay awhile longer at the haven. Wants to take me on a tour of Edinburgh."

I gave him a huge smile. "That's great. Are you going to take her up on it?"

He nodded and looked at the ground.

I gave him another nudge. "She's very sweet, but kind of old school. Maybe you can bring her into the twenty-first century. Buy her some skinny jeans and a T-shirt."

"Ha! I seriously doubt that will ever happen." We both burst out laughing, leaning into one another. Eventually, our giggles died off and he rose to his feet. "Speaking of Teresa, I'm meeting her in the blood lounge. Better get going. Are you coming in?"

I took in a breath of night air and looked up at the stars. "I'm fine right here for the moment."

He seemed to drink me in with his eyes for another moment, then finally said, "Okay. Good night then."

"Good night," I said, watching until he vanished inside the haven doors.

As I sat under the moonlight my gaze wandered about the garden, and I was revisited by the past. My life had been far from straightforward, full of twists and turns, never a dull moment. As an infant, I was traded away by my own mother and abandoned by my father. My hand had been promised to a vampire god as if I'd lived in an era when arranged marriages were commonplace. Throughout my childhood, teenage, and adult years, a mysterious mist had showered me with undying love. I'd broken the heart of one friend and ended the life of another, transformed into some kind of hybrid being: half-human and half-vampire creature. I'd been shot through the heart by a crazed lunatic and nearly died. To escape death, I'd consumed the blood of a vampire and become a full vampire myself. I survived not one, but two binding rituals. All that had happened in the span of my first thirty years, and I still had all of eternity stretched out before me. What else could possibly befall me during that unlimited amount of time? I stretched my arms overhead and turned my attention again to the beautiful starlit sky. Just like Scarlett O'Hara, I'd think about any troubles tomorrow.

"There you are," Amon called from a distance.

I turned toward the magic that was his voice and saw him halfway down the brick walkway. He waved and jogged the short distance to reach me. He brought my hand to his lips and kissed it when he sat beside me. "I got tired of waiting."

"I'm sorry. There was Danny and then Philippe. I needed a moment to breathe."

"How did everything go with the two of them?"

I snuggled up to him and rested my head on his shoulder. "Danny's a professor at a university; The Council gave him a brand-new life. And Philippe finally agreed we were over. I forgave him...*and* he's sweet on Teresa."

"Wow. A lot's happened since you left me in bed." He lifted my chin to examine my eyes. "Are you okay?"

"I'm good. All is right with the world again. But where do we go from here?"

He scooted a little closer and held me a little tighter. "We'll go home."

"An empty home." I pointed out. Castle Beach, with its crashing waves and ocean air, appeared ordinary weighed against London's foggy streets and mist-kissed skies, or Edinburgh's green mountain tops covered in ancient castles...The Council's haven being one of them. But I felt secure within its boundaries. It was my home.

He chuckled and gave me a playful squeeze. "We'll fill it with furniture. We'll spend every day completely and passionately in love with each other. We'll make love all day and drink blood all night. We'll just enjoy life."

I looked up at him and, basking in the glow of his gorgeous emerald-green eyes, I avowed, "Forever and ever."

He kissed me on the forehead, nose, each cheek, and finally on my lips before he echoed my words with pure conviction. "Forever and ever."

About the Author

LAURA DALEO is a multi-genre author, specializing in Dark Fantasy, Urban Fantasy, Supernatural Fiction, Science Fiction, and Young Adult Fiction. Immortal Kiss, her best-known vampire series, explores the Egyptian pantheon that gave rise to vampires. Currently, she is working on her eighth book.

A native of San Diego, California, Laura now lives in Tucson, Arizona with her two dogs, Rose and Cooper.